The Year of EVERYTHING

CAT PORTER

WILDFLOWER INK, LLC

The Year of Everything
Cat Porter ©2019
Wildflower Ink, LLC

Editor
Jennifer Roberts-Hall

Cover Designer
Cat Porter & Lori Jackson Design

Cover Photographer
Collins Lesulie on Unsplash

Proofreader
Jenni McCoy Alford

Visit my website at www.catporter.eu

ISBN: 978-1-954633-02-5

Prologue

WHEN I WALKED up the steps to Meager Senior High that September morning, I had no idea that by the end of the year, my life as I knew it would be over.

Every high school senior anticipates having their best year ever. I certainly did. I had good grades going in, an SAT prep course under my belt, I was a yearbook editor, I knew which university I wanted to go to, had money in my pocket from my crappy summer job. Great friends. A guy who liked me and who I liked too.

Senior year, here I come. Watch out for Grace Hastings!

I had everything going for me.

Only, the everything I thought I knew was wrong.

Everything I believed in wasn't real.

Everything I was holding onto up until that moment turned out to be meaningless.

Well, no. That was a bit dramatic, wasn't it?

This was more accurate—everything could crack, break, shatter. Crash. Flip the fuck over and burn.

And it did.

Chapter One

"YOU'RE LATE! Come on, come on. Move to the back against the wall. Let's go!" The math teacher, Mr. Raines, motioned for all us latecomers to stand at the back. We'd already trudged through two weeks of the new school year, and this was our first assembly.

My lucky day.

First, I'd had to take the school bus this morning—total humiliation—because my sister, Ruby, who let me use her car on occasion, hadn't gone to the gas station last night to fill it up like she'd promised. Then I found out I'd gotten switched into Mr. Raines for math. Mr. Raines liked to hear himself talk and explain theory, but that didn't help me figure out his homework assignments.

"Hush now!" came Raines's stern voice as Principal Powers spoke from the podium on stage. The school choir was lined up behind him. *Great. Another classic "Welcome Back to Meager High" production. Sniff, sniff, my last September assembly.*

My body got shoved into the big guy next to me, and I turned to the idiot on my other side who'd done the shoving, a football player in his Varsity T-shirt. "Hey!"

"Sorry, Grace." Manny shrugged and went back to

making fun of the choir's rendition of the Star-Spangled Banner with his buddy.

Mr. Raines directed more stragglers to our wall, like an airplane traffic guy on the tarmac waving wands. We all shuffled to make room, appeasing him. I attempted to adjust myself, and my bare arm brushed the guy's on the other side of me. Warm silk. Holding my breath, I inched back from him as far as I could, but there was nowhere else to go, I was stuck. Stuck against the cold wall, stuck against him. I swallowed hard and breathed in a new scent that circled me like a tightening lasso—freshly cut wood laced with cigarette smoke.

Lava-like heat suddenly flowed through my body, and I kept still as my breaths picked up speed. My gaze darted down, following that long arm to a big hand that held onto two textbooks covered in crinkly brown shopping bag paper like mine. Mine had Springsteen lyrics which I'd proudly penned from memory, but his—his blazed with amazing colored drawings, like some pricey, professional comic book. Swirling dragons and comets exploding, alien creatures flying, vibrant whirls of rich electric color visible in the half-light.

I bent my head to see more in a glow of light from the open doorway to the hall. There was something dark and forbidding about his art, but earnest too. *I believe,* the insistent drive of color and shape declared to me. *I am here. My voice. Hear me. Me.*

I blinked, stealing a glance at him. Two grim black eyes stared back at me, and my pulse jumped. Words were suddenly beyond me, and I offered him a smile. His features softened for a split second, and my smile widened, but he looked away, his face neutral once more, stony. The hot rays of his sun were suddenly blocked by clouds, and I stood alone in their shade.

I dug a foot back up against the wall to keep my balance. Miss Cool. Trying hard to keep my focus on the stage, on the choir, the cheerleaders while being sandwiched between

Manny's jostling and stupid commentary on one side, and Dark and Intriguing Silent Artist on the other.

Applause. Whoops. Another announcement about the first football game of the season and the scheduled pep rally. Homecoming is ahead of us. Rah-rah, Meager Mustangs! More whoops and hoots. Assembly over. *Finally.* I shot off the wall, diving into the river of chaos and noise spilling out into the hallway.

I hustled to Tania's locker, where I knew she'd be. "Hey."

"Ugh, that choir." Tania struggled with a pile of books and her handbag in her locker.

"I know, right?" I murmured.

"You know how I have Coach Hildebrand for Health? Today is going to be epic. Him explaining ovulation—priceless. Plus, I have half the football team in my class…"

There he is. That's him.

At the end of Tania's section, there he stood, opening his locker. Long, black hair in his face, tall and lean, curves of muscle obvious under his white T-shirt. Bright white cotton against dark skin. Dark and smooth. I may have felt the sensation of that skin against mine about half an hour ago, but the memory was still fresh, goosebumps prickled my skin once more. I shifted my weight, chewing on my lip as my gaze trailed down his long legs cased in faded jeans. He wasn't wearing sneakers or cowboy boots like the rest of us, but thick, square-cut black boots. The kind guys who rode motorcycles wore. Did he have his own bike? If he didn't, he definitely should.

He shook his head as he leaned to the side, zipping up his backpack, and that glossy, dark hair skimmed past his shoulder. Something warm shimmied through my middle and pulled, and in that pull, I saw him riding a motorcycle at top speed, that hair flying behind him, the hard pitch of his groaning engine ripping through Meager—

"Hey? Grace? What the heck are you staring at?"

My head snapped back toward Tania. "Huh?" My gaze darted back to him rummaging through his locker, and that clean yet smoky, mystery man scent along with his moody eyes haunted me in a rush, pricking at my senses all over again like a hundred thorns.

Tania bumped my hip with hers, and I tore my gaze away from Tall, Dark, and Intriguing. A smirk twitched her lips.

I flicked my hair over my shoulder. "What? Nothing, just—"

"Just?" Her gaze darted to where mine had lingered for so long, her eyes suddenly widening. "Gotcha, girlfriend."

I edged closer to her. "You can't say he's not super cute."

"That's not all I'd say, but yeah. He's a total babe." Tania went back to getting her books in order.

"You know, my locker's all the way down the other end of the hall," I said. "And you've been getting to check him out since school started two weeks ago, and you haven't said a word. Not a word. What kind of best friend are you?"

Tania let out a laugh. "Okay, he's nice to look at, but not my speed."

My fingers ran through the ends of my hair. "He's new, isn't he?"

"Yeah. Haven't you seen him around town before? I have."

I shrugged. "I guess. We stood next to each other at the assembly in the back and—"

"And you ovulated?"

"Shut up."

"Ah!" Her eyes widened dramatically. "You had an anonymous Penthouse encounter?"

"Stop!" I laughed.

Tania had found her uncle's stash of Penthouse magazines in her grandmother's attic over the summer, and we'd had a field day going through them one night with a six-pack of beer.

"You cradle robber. He's a sophomore or maybe, a junior, I'm not sure." Tania shut her locker door and twisted the combo lock.

I crossed my arms around my chemistry books, pulling them up against my chest. "Really? He's so tall … you'd think he was older."

"It's that serious look on his face. Word is that he's related to one of the One-Eyed Jacks."

"No way."

"Yes way. His older brother is a Jack, and he moved here from Pine Ridge to live with him."

"Hmm." He was Native American all right, but not one hundred percent. He turned, and I noticed a thin necklace made of colored beads around his neck. My teeth scraped my bottom lip. Guys with jewelry. It had to be the right jewelry, though. That necklace looked good on him. It looked right.

"You should ask Ruby about him." Tania's grin twisted into a scowl. "Bet she'd know all the deets."

My sister, Ruby, had been up at the Jacks's clubhouse at the edge of town this past Saturday night for some party they were having. It was her first biker party, and her first time up at the One-Eyed Jacks clubhouse. Tania had been horrified. I'd been somewhat fascinated.

"Are you sure you want to go?" I'd asked Ruby as she was getting dressed for the party.

"Are you kidding? I've been dying to go all summer. Perfect timing since Dad's out of town for the weekend, so…"

Ruby had graduated high school two years ago but still lived at home. For now.

"Yeah, but aren't the Jacks older and really wild?"

"I hope so." She'd laughed to herself in that throaty, wicked way that always had me gritting my teeth. She snapped on her black bra. "Not *all* of them are older. They're real men, Grace. They know how to party."

"I'll bet they do. You're coming home tonight, right?"

"I don't know..." Ruby fitted her tight blouse over her ripped jeans, threw on some makeup, heels, and flew out of the house.

Later that night, when our mother had come home from dinner and drinks with friends, she'd asked me where Ruby was. *"She's spending the night at Katie's house, Ma." Lie, lie, lie.*

Luckily Ruby had come home, but at four in the morning, barreling through my bedroom window, stinking of pot, cigarettes, and hard booze. I'd gotten her out of her clothes, and she'd curled up next to me in my bed and babbled about men with beards and crazy tattoos all over their bodies.

"So sexy. Oh my God." She'd curled into the pillow on a drawn-out groan.

I was intrigued as if she were recounting some sort of exotic fantasy thriller. She'd told me everything, too. She always did.

"So, did you fool around with a Jack?"

"No, dammit. They all seemed to have girlfriends, plus there were lots of biker chicks there, all trying to get their attention, and fuck, they were so bitchy to us townies, and you wanna know why? 'Cause we're young and fine, that's why. Next time, though. Next time for sure..."

"Shh! Shut up already," I'd whispered through my laughter. "Mom's going to hear."

I'd been relieved Ruby had come home because if she'd gone missing, it would become a thing between Dad and Mom, alleged sleepover or no sleepover. Our parents fought over everything these days.

The next period bell rang, and my body jerked off the bank of lockers, bringing me back to Tania and the brutal reality of chemistry class.

"Let's go," said Tania. "Time for torture by isotope." We turned down the hallway toward class.

"Hey, babes." Mike came up beside me, slinging an arm around my shoulder. "Going my way?"

I smiled at him, my fingers tightening over my books. "I think so." Mike and I had hung out together at a bunch of parties over the summer. He'd driven me home once, and we'd kissed. He was a nice guy. He played football and wanted to be a doctor like his dad.

I walked on with Tania and Mike, but my gaze darted over my shoulder, back to *him*.

But he wasn't there.

Chapter Two

"GO, Big Red! Fight, Big White! Do it, do it, all right, all right!" We pounded the bleachers jumping up and down, repeating our Meager High spirit chant, or whatever it was called. Now, as seniors, it was ingrained in us.

We'd stumbled into October already. The regular pep rallies in the school gym for the upcoming football game allowed us to go a little wild after a day of slogging through our classes and finishing up another week.

The varsity lineup was being introduced, and Tania poked me in the side with her elbow. "Number 33, Miller LeBeau!" said Coach Hildebrand into the microphone at the podium that was way too short for him.

It was the new guy. He was on the team now.

Miller rose from his chair standing stiffly, his face frozen into a look of alarm and discomfort. The cheerleaders shook their red and white pompoms in the air, and we all clapped and cheered loudly. Eyes wide, he sat down right away.

"Made the varsity football team in time for Homecoming? Well, well, well," murmured Tania.

"Now she notices him," I said.

"Mike Dubransky, number 18!" announced Coach Hildebrand.

My clapping wasn't as enthusiastic this time. Although Mike was cute and nice and funny, I wasn't feeling *it, not really.* Ever since school had started, he'd been pushing. The other day he'd given me a ride home after we'd bumped into each other in town, and when he realized my parents' cars weren't in the driveway, he'd wanted to come inside. I told him no, mom was definitely home, that her car was in the shop. He'd been super disappointed, and we kissed quickly, a few swipes of tongue. I got out of his Bronco real fast.

Last Saturday we'd gone to a party together and ended up fooling around, and he'd fingered me. I think I came, I wasn't really sure. It was something, though, and Mike was super pleased with himself. I knew the next time we'd be alone, fooling around, he'd want to go further. Clothes would come off. But I really didn't want to go further, and his laser beam attention was making me uncomfortable. I was going to have to finally open my mouth and tell him I wasn't into him. Or something.

"When he asks you to Homecoming, what are you going to say?" Tania asked.

I let out a groan. "I don't know."

"You don't know?"

"Go, Big Red! Fight, Big White! Do it, do it, all right, all right!"

I don't want to do it. Not with Mike. I let out a breath to release the knot in my gut as the chanting intensified, reverberating through that buckling knot.

Tania leaned into me. "You going to let him score a touchdown on your field?"

"He got as far as a first down."

"Yep, and what's a few more yard lines?" Tania let out a laugh.

"And your quarterback, number 45—" Coach Hildebrand's voice soared. He was the master of ceremonies under the spotlight of an arena. "Marshall Hildebrand!" he drew out the name.

The crowd went apeshit, the noise thundering in the gym. Marshall was Coach's nephew, and Coach Hildy's whole face was like a high beam headlight as he clapped and whooped along with the crowd. Marshall, tall, blond, and blue-eyed, waved both his long buff arms up in the air. His hands fisted and pumped along with the chanting of "Mar-shall! Mar-shall!" He loved the hero worship, that was for sure.

The band exploded into a triumphant blast of horns, brass, and drums, buoying Marshall and the team even higher. The cheerleaders charged from the sidelines, tumbling and hopping on top of each other. My adrenaline pumped along with each shout and whoop. This mass enthusiasm was powerful stuff. Coach Hildy went on and on about how we were going to *crush* Belton High, *pulverize* them. When he was impassioned, he was articulate, dramatic. In health class, though, he was pretty damned passive, but he had a dry sense of humor, which made up for it.

"Erica's got it bad," I said to Tania.

"I know, right?"

Erica Drake was a senior like Tania and me, and she was a cheerleader. Her partner threw her in the air, and she tumbled and flipped back into his embrace like a pro. Her beauty pageant smile gave way to darting glances at our quarterback.

"Ever since she and Marshall had that make out sesh at Sandy's party a couple of weeks ago, they've been hanging out," said Tania.

"He's that good of a kisser, huh?"

"Nah, I kissed him, remember?"

"That was in the third grade." I let out a laugh, shoving at her with my shoulder.

"Dude! How can you forget that Valentine's Day Dance freshman year?"

"Oh my God, right, but you were both drunk."

"So? I still remember it. Blech. Some guys think using their tongue like an electric power drill is impressive. Idiots. No sense of the sensual. But I have to say, his hands sure knew what to do."

"Well, look at our football hero now. The whole package in blazing glory. He's got it all. That hair, those eyes, that bod."

"That car."

"The money."

"And the attitude to go with all of it."

The Hildebrand family went back a long way in the Black Hills. Lawyers, realtors, bankers. They did it all, and they owned a hell of a lot more. On the other hand, Erica's family, the Drakes, had run the humble coffee shop in town for generations, and her mother's side of the family owned the old general store in Meager—the five and dime as we'd always called it. Growing up, my sister and I would run there with our allowance money and buy candy, and more recently, an inexpensive lipgloss or nail polish. It was every Meager mom's go-to for socks, greeting cards, gift wrap, Halloween costumes, and holiday decorations, to name but a few. There was always something to buy at Dillon's General Store.

The pep rally was over, so we all clamored down from the bleachers toward the exit. "Hey, Erica!" called out Tania, waving her hand. "Looking good."

"Thanks." Erica brushed her bangs from her red face. "You coming to the game tonight, right? We're all heading to Frank's for pizza after." Frank's was a pizzeria in Rapid that we all liked and usually went to after a game at the stadium there.

"Are you kidding?" I said. "Wouldn't miss it."

Chapter Three

WE WON THE FOOTBALL GAME, 10-3. The crowd went wild. We spilled our sodas. In fact, everyone was spilling their sodas, popcorn flying as we all jumped up and down in the bleachers. Our Meager Mustang mascot danced wildly on the field with the cheerleaders, the marching band's brass and drums exploding along with our adrenaline. We were on top of the world.

Everyone headed to Frank's afterward. Of course, the real party wasn't inside the pizzeria, but outside in the parking lot. A bunch of us were hanging on the hood of Tania's car. Tania had brought a mini bottle of rum and had been adding it to our colas. "Who wants another Mur & Bats?"

"I'm good," I said. My knees were already rubbery.

"What's Mur & Bats?" asked Erica.

"It's Rum & Tab," I replied on a laugh. "Tania loves thinking up these clever ditties in her attempts to hide her illicit activities from her mom."

"I'm drinking a Sprite, though," said Erica.

"So what, I'll add some Mur, how's that?" Tania took out our small bottle of rum from her car.

"I guess." Erica laughed. She opened the plastic lid of her

drink, and Tania poured in the rum. Erica swirled the cup, replaced the lid, and sipped on her straw once more. "Oh. Nice."

"That's it." Tania tucked the bottle back in the car.

"That's good," said Erica.

"What's good?" came a deep voice from behind us. We all turned. Marshall Hildebrand, Mike, Manny, and two of their buddies stood there, drinking from open plastic cups.

"Oh, hey." Erica grinned. "Tania brought some magic juice to the party, that's all."

"Oh yeah?" Marshall's lips swerved into a sexy grin. "I want to try." His fingers slid around Erica's drink cup, touching her fingers, and her lips parted.

"Sure, go ahead." Erica's voice was suddenly breathy.

His gaze flicked over Tania and me, then went back to Erica. Taking a sip from her straw, his eyes widened for a moment, another grin growing on his attractive mouth.

"Good, right?" Erica said over the noise of cars driving by.

Marshall licked his upper lip, and Erica took in a deep breath at the sight. He handed her back her drink. "Aren't you the wild girl, huh?" His fingers ruffled through her ponytail, and her back straightened, her neck arched. She was a kitten in his hands. I'd bet she was all goosebumps and tingles.

Marshall released her hair, making it swing over her back. He smirked, his gaze lingering on her. Erica was spellbound. He leaned over and whispered in her ear. Her eyes fluttered for a moment, and she gripped her cup tightly. He pulled back and squeezed her arm. Erica smiled lazily at him as she sipped on her drink. She'd been entranced by Marshall Magic. His look, his touch. His spit on her straw.

"Hey, you." A hand crawled up my back, and I flinched. Mike. His eyes were glassy, his tongue rubbing at his bottom lip. It was a habit of his. A habit that I didn't like much.

I shifted my weight under his intense, expectant stare. "Hey. Great game." My back stiffened under his roving hand.

"Yeah, thanks." His arm circled my shoulders, pulling me into him. "You doing good? You look good." His weight fell on me, his beer breath warm and humid on my face.

"Um, yeah … thanks."

"What are you doing after this?"

"Going home."

"We're gonna go to Marshall's house and play some pinball and shit. Hang out, you know. His parents are in Vegas this weekend." He pointed his beer can at Erica. "Erica's coming. You should come with her. We could hang."

Hang. Yeah.

"Uh—"

He nuzzled the side of my face, leaving traces of beer and saliva behind. "What do you say?"

"Let's go, dude," said Marshall.

"Yep." Mike released me and stalked off with Marshall and the rest of their crew. Over his shoulder, Marshall shot Erica a wink and a grin.

A rare silence remained as we all admired our quarterback strut away. I finally understood how a guy's rear end could be perfection in the right pair of jeans.

"So Erica, what's the deal with you and Marshall?" Tania's voice shook me from my fog.

"What deal?" said Erica, brushing back her wispy bangs from her eyes.

"You like him, don't you?" Tania continued, her voice morphing into her tight brand of sarcasm.

"Yep," Erica's eyes glimmered as she sipped her drink. "We sit next to each other in History. We talk … he's funny. He's…"

"He's sexy as hell," declared Tania.

The three of us exploded into laughter.

"You two look good together." I touched Erica's arm. "He obviously likes you."

Erica grinned. "I like him, too. A lot."

"Have you gone out and stuff?"

"A couple times. We hang out before practice sometimes."

"Ooo. Has he asked you to Homecoming?"

"Tan, relax," I said.

"What? I'm rooting for Erica here."

"Yes, he asked me," Erica replied.

"Oh my God, all right!" whooped Tania.

"Wow," I added. "You said yes, right?"

"You bet I said yes," Erica said. "Are you guys going?"

"We'll be at the bonfire." I shrugged.

"Oh, I thought maybe you and Mike…" Erica started. "But I can't see you together."

"Really? Why?"

"Your eyes don't light up when he's around," said Erica.

"They don't, huh?"

"You don't like him like he likes you. Simple as that." Erica sucked on her drink.

"It should be simple, right? I mean, I like him, but I don't get goosebumps or breathless or any of that stuff. That super intense crush stuff. I want to feel that. I want to know what that's like."

"I think Erica knows what that's like," Tania said.

Erica turned bright red, nodding, grinning.

"That's great." I leaned back against Tania's car. "Am I just being too picky? I don't know. Sometimes I find myself thinking maybe I'm being stubborn, you know?"

Erica's straw made a harsh noise. She shook her ice-filled cup. "Oh." Her drink was gone.

"I'd like to fool around with some hunk and then walk away. Can't I do that?" said Tania. "Guys do it."

"Sure," I said. "I wouldn't say no to that either."

"But without them thinking that you're on tap for them after. No, sorry, dude. Done," Tania added.

"You guys crack me up." Erica laughed.

I let out a sigh. "Your eyes lit up when Marshall was here, Erica. And in Marshall, you've got the sexy boy *and* the perfect boy your parents would want you to like all rolled into one. Lucky you." Tania and I clinked our cups with hers. "Mike said that they're all going over to Marshall's tonight to hang out," I said to Erica. "Are you going?"

"Yeah, he invited me." She was beaming. "Actually—" She checked her watch. "I need to get going. I'm meeting up with them at Marshall's car." She scanned the parking lot. "There they are. Thanks for the Mur & Bats, you guys."

"Anytime," said Tania.

"Have fun," I said.

"Bye." Erica waved at us as she took off toward the Marshall mobile.

I checked my own watch. "Oh, brother, I have to get home. The stupid payphone here is busted again, and I told my dad I'd check in—I could have maybe wrangled another half hour, but now he's going to have my hide if I'm not home by eleven-thirty on the dot."

"Ooooh, so you could go to Marshall's and wrangle Mike?" Tania's eyebrows wobbled.

"Yeah, right."

"He likes you so much. He's cute and kinda hunky. Think of it—homecoming with an actual football player. Kinda great. You could double date with Captain and Miss America." She gestured toward Erica, who was dashing over to Marshall.

"I guess."

"You guess?"

"I like him. I do. But, like Erica said, I'm not getting goosebumpy over him, you know?"

"Scarlet O'Hara didn't get goosebumpy over Rhett Butler at first either. Only annoyed. And see how that turned out?"

"Oh no, no, no. Scarlet got goosebumpy, all right, but she was in total denial and totally stubborn."

"Good point. Well, see, you may be in denial too. You do have a stubborn streak. Bottom line, you'll never know unless you give it a chance. What have you got to lose? Ah! Your virginity."

"Shut up."

Tania let out a laugh as she slid off the hood of her car. "Your dad knows you're with me. What's the big deal?"

"It's not that. A couple of weeks ago, he spotted Ruby at Dead Ringer's dancing with some biker."

"No way. Was it a Jack?"

"No, some out of town bikers passing through."

"Well, you go to Dead Ringers Saloon to meet cowboys and bikers. Geez, her fake ID is amazing."

"I know, right? Anyhow, forget it, Dad's been buckling down on me ever since. It's been lots of fun at our house lately." *Isn't it always?*

"As if you're like Ruby." Tania rolled her eyes. "Give me a break."

I let out a groan. "Sometimes, I wish I was more like my sister. Loud, tough, in your face. Doing what she wants and not giving a shit. Taking off without a look back. Having her fun without considering tomorrow."

"You think too much."

I couldn't help it. I always imagined all the angles of a situation and what the other person must be thinking and feeling. It was a lot of noise in my head. Noise that led to me confusing what I wanted with what I should do.

Or something.

Chapter Four

THINGS between my mom and dad had heated up. Actually, they had iced down to the point where my mother muttered to herself in the kitchen over a cigarette while dad took off more often by taking on more delivery jobs, so he was absent more than he was home. Ruby and I had gotten used to it. We shouldn't have, though. It should have felt unusual. Wrong, even. Like something was missing.

Someone was missing.

Ever since our little brother, Jason, got run over by a car and killed about five years ago, nothing had been the same at home. Dad shut down. Mom had no place to land. Ruby got wilder, louder.

And me? I held the pole in the center of the circus tent that was our family. No one knew how to reach out. To communicate. I could see the careless mistakes we were all making, but I felt powerless to do anything about it. And no one seemed willing to try.

So I cooked dinner when Mom would forget or didn't feel up to it, kept the bathroom clean, made sure the garbage was dealt with, that we had toilet paper and laundry detergent. All the little things that kept the tent standing through the winds and the rain.

I was never under the illusion that my parents had some big romantic love story going on. They'd married young when Mom got pregnant with Ruby. And the loss of Jason had ripped open the patches they'd slapped on the rips and the cracks over the years. Now their hurt was too deep, too raw, and always would be.

Ruby and I were go with the flow types. We didn't fight the waves of the sea. Through every pull and tug of the wild current, we held on. Through every smack of icy cold water, we held onto each other. Spitting out the water we accidentally swallowed, we held on. We'd learned to suck it up, because otherwise, our floating days were numbered, and there were no rescue boats in sight.

Ruby had a steady job at a restaurant in Rapid as a hostess, and she worked at another bar on the weekends. She made enough in tips to keep her happy, but she was saving money to move to an apartment in Rapid. I was glad for her. All she ever wanted was to be on her own to do her thing.

Ultimately, what she wanted was to go to Colorado and live with Keith, one of her best friends from high school. He worked in some trendy, underground hair salon out there and deejayed at a nightclub. Ruby was eager to get on with her life and live large. I knew she would flourish no matter what she did. She had so much personality, so much determination. How could she not live the large she wanted so badly?

If only I knew what I wanted.

Mike asked me to Homecoming, and I said yes.

"YES!" He picked me up and whirled me around, and my heart jammed up my throat for a painful second. "We're going to have a blast. Total blast." There would be parties with all the other players and their girlfriends the weekend before and after. At least I knew Erica.

After a week of Homecoming brouhaha at school where

we all wore our school colors or T-shirts every day of the week, the game finally arrived, and the dance that night. Marshall had been crowned king, and the queen was Cindy, the captain of the girl's volleyball team. At the bonfire the night before the game, he was making out with Erica, and I took an amazing photo of them for the yearbook. I was on the yearbook editing team, and I'd get that pic in there, make it bigger than the one with Marshall and Cindy.

There was a full moon that night, and after the dance, Mike brought me to Hot Springs, where we were going to hang out at the reservoir for a couple of hours with a bunch of other couples, but there was no sign of anyone anywhere.

Mike pulled his car to a stop in front of a small wood cabin.

"What's this?" My back stiffened against the curve of my seat.

"It's Larry's dad's fishing cabin. We're all meeting here. Larry's got the keys, of course, so we need to wait for him and Staci to get here."

A tide of seawater flooded me, and I took a quick breath to push back from the threatening wave. "I don't understand. You never said—"

"Manny and Susan are already here—" He pointed to the red pickup truck parked farther down. Manny and Susan were one single shadowy figure moving in the cab of the truck. My mouth dried, my stomach curled.

Mike's hand pressed down my thigh over my dark rose-colored dress. His fingers crept under the hem, tucked under the waistband of my panties.

"Mike—"

He was in, fingers searching, grazing. His eyebrows lifted, his jaw dropping open, face pressed against mine. "Yeah..." Triumph. His tongue swiped at the corner of my mouth, leaving that patch of my face wet.

"Wait—" I twisted away from him. "Can you—"

"Come on, Grace. We're always fooling around in my car. Tonight, we got our own room at the cabin all to ourselves. I can't wait…" He twisted his hand between my legs. "Oh yeahhhh … there…" his fingers rubbed stiffly against my clit. "Yeahhhh," he repeated, his tongue swiping at my jawline. My hand cuffed his wrist, and I grit my teeth.

"Can't wait to get you alone. Tonight we're going to finally do it, huh?" he muttered against my skin.

"Mike—"

"Fuck, I'm so hard." He clutched at my hand, placing it on top of his erection, squeezing. "I brought rubbers, so don't worry."

Don't worry? Don't worry?

A brick wall of panic slammed up my chest and cut off my breath. He ground his pelvis against my hand, his fingers between my legs rough, and my whole body went stiff, bracing. *Stop, stop, stop,* rumbled through me. His hand, clutching mine at his crotch, only grew tighter.

I didn't like this.

I didn't want this.

I hated this.

"Mike. Mike!" My voice grew stronger as he chewed on my throat.

"Oh shit, I think I came. Dammit." He let out a low chuckle, releasing my hand as he raised his hips, adjusting his pants.

My body pressed back against the door. "Mike. I-I don't want to spend the night here."

"What?" He smoothed a hand down his trousers.

"I don't want to spend the—"

"What? Why not?"

"I don't want to … have sex with you tonight."

"What are you talking about? I thought you were into it?"

"Um, yeah, I am—"

"So?" His eyes tightened. He was angry.

"But—"

"But what?" The look on his face made my skin tighten. His eyes shot hot lasers at me, lasers meant to burn. To put me on the spot. Mike was in offensive mode.

"We never said…"

"Are you kidding me? Come on, wasn't it obvious?"

"No, not to me."

"What?" His face creased into a bitter grimace. I was speaking a foreign language and it was annoying.

"You can't assume that—"

"Hold on. You're telling me you're not going to sleep with me tonight?" We stared at each other in the dark of his car, the air thick, the low lights from the cabin pathway glimmering over our faces. He leaned into me, jaw jutting, lips snarling. "Are you ever?"

Whoa, that wasn't a simple question, it was a dare. A humiliation. Mine.

My stomach cramped painfully. My fingers curled in the fabric of my dress. If only my flimsy dress were armor. Did I owe him sex? Is that what he thought all along?

"This was gonna be an amazing senior year for us, Grace." His voice flared as he pushed back in his seat. "Come on!"

My jaw hardened, and I braced my throat, my tongue against the words, *"I'm sorry,"* which brewed there. My pulse pounded. Adrenaline. To get out of the car? To run? *Say it. Say it. Say it.*

"I don't want to sleep with you tonight, Mike."

"I don't believe this shit," he spit out. "What the fuck?"

I shrank by the car door, the metal handle cold against my bare arm. He continued to mutter under his breath. My hand bunched in my dress. The dress I'd overspent on and Ruby had helped me pay for. The dress I loved. Burning heat flared over my skin. Dress of shame.

No. I am not feeling bad or guilty about this. Did he ask me? No. He assumed. He brought me up here, expecting me to ... He fucking cornered me. I sucked in a tight breath for sanity's sake.

"You know, I thought we had something here, Grace. I thought you liked me. Like *really* liked me."

"Could you take me home, please?"

Chapter Five

I DIDN'T GET out of bed the next morning.

My door burst open. A thwack on my butt. "Ow!" My quilt was ripped off me, down the bed. "Leave me alone."

"What happened?" said Ruby, throwing herself on my bed.

"Nothing."

"Tell me."

I told her.

"Dick. Total fucking dick."

"I feel like an idiot."

"You're not an idiot."

"Well, I feel like one."

"Why?"

"We've been fooling around … I should have realized or something."

"You should have *realized?* Realized what? That after a certain number of kisses and gropes, you had to have sex with him? Gracie, if you're not feeling it, you're not feeling it, end of story. He knew it too, so he tried to force your hand. Taking you to that cabin … get fucking real. He planned this all along."

"Don't make him out to be this evil guy, Rube."

"Fine, he's not evil, he's just a dick making a dick move."

I twisted my fingers in my sheet, letting my gaze wander out of my window.

"Grace?" She squeezed my leg. "I'm glad you're okay."

"When will I know, Rube? Huh? When will I know that I'm with the right guy?"

"You're asking me?" She smirked.

"Yes."

"You'll know. Anyhow, you've got years and years ahead of you to kiss a lot of frogs as they say. And you will. I don't know if there's any such thing as Mr. Right, or The One, or your soul mate. I know you think so—"

"I do."

She tucked her hands under her head. "It'd be nice. But I don't think it's that simple."

"I want to feel something big and have the guy feel the same way. Some kind of real emotion and intense attraction. The I-can't-breathe-body-melting-heart-banging-in-my-chest-I-want-you-so-bad kind. Not just *hey, let's do it.*"

Ruby only laughed.

"I'm asking for too much, huh?"

"I'm not laughing at you. I get it. I know I used to tease you about losing it, but if you want something more your first time, like you said, then wait for the right guy. One day there will be a ton of guys you'll want to screw and not be in a relationship with."

"Look," I adjusted myself on my pillow. "I'm not saying I have to be in love with a guy to do it, but I don't want my first time to be a throwaway with just anybody to get it over with or say that I did it. I want it to be good, special, not some sloppy—"

"Like me?"

"Hey, you still laugh over you and that jerk, whatshisname,

doing it in his truck in the snow, freezing your asses off, no room to move. You didn't even like him that much."

Ruby stretched out. "He gave me a ride home from school, and we got stuck in that snowstorm. He was cute. I knew he liked me, and I figured why the hell not. It was an opportunity. Definitely wasn't memorable, though."

"I don't want just some opportunity. I don't want to laugh about it or roll my eyes later. Sorry."

"You don't have to be sorry. I get it, Gracie. I do."

We both stared up at the ceiling. The radio in the kitchen blasted Bon Jovi's Lay Your Hands on Me, and we groaned and giggled.

"Forget Mike," said Ruby. "If you want to wait for The One, Grace, do it. But don't bow out of the game, because you have to be in it to win it."

"Win?"

"Get what you want"—Ruby turned over on the bed, her head in her hand, her gaze going out the window—"the way you want it."

———

Mike avoided me like I was a disease for which there was no vaccine. He'd see me down the hall and zip off in another direction. Then that turned to hard glances meant to communicate disdain and bitterness. Eventually, all of that morphed to complete ignoring.

Whatever.

I focused on studying and getting my college essay right. Midterms. Finals. Thanksgiving, Christmas break. So much snow.

In February, Dad got stuck in a blizzard in Wyoming and didn't come home for a whole week. Meager had basically shut down, and Mom declared it was Girls' Night and made us a macaroni and cheese and bacon casserole, which we ate in the living room in our fleece pajamas and robes watching a new TV show, "Baywatch." Oh, to live the LA life—have a perfect bikini bod and swim at the sunny beach all year round.

Come late March, spring had most certainly sprung, and we natives were cranky. Even if a weekend turned cold and snowy, the next would be super warm and sunny. A few eager citizens of Meager had already stepped out in shorts and fished out their Birkenstocks from the back of their closets. Bikers were zipping around again and in tank tops. There was excitement in the air.

Tania and I had taken an SAT class over the summer because, when we first took the test last year, our scores had sucked googooballs. We'd felt much better about the test the second time around. My grades were good, and I had high hopes. I wanted to go to Denver, to the University of Colorado. I could swing it if I got a job or two. It was my number one choice. Second choice was the University of SD in Vermillion. The money I'd need there would be on the much lower side, and I'd be closer to home, but I wanted that far away from home college experience.

Tania had been accepted into the University of Chicago early. She'd gotten a good financial aid package, and a great aunt of hers, who was unmarried and had money, had promised her some funds too. Tania was from a farm family, and she'd be the first one to go to college. I was going to miss her. We'd been together at school since Pre-K. But we were adults now, weren't we? We had different interests, we'd make different inlays on different roads, and that was exciting. That was life. We'd see each other on holidays at home, and I was already making plans in my head to visit her in Chicago. I couldn't even imagine a big city like Chicago.

I got home from school and found the mail dumped on the kitchen table. Electric bill, coupon junk mail, an Easter promo flyer from Dillon's, an envelope from the University of Denver.

OH MY GOD.

My knees locking, I pulled in a tight breath as my fingers pressed over the envelope. My mouth dried as I tucked my thumbnail under the flap and ripped ripped ripped. What would I find? My whole life lay in that thick fold of papers. A tremor shook through me. I opened up the papers, sucking in the black printed words on the letter.

"We are pleased to inform you…"

I swallowed the words whole. I read it again.

I've been accepted. I've been accepted. Oh my God, I'm going to Denver!

My heart exploded against my ribs like a bull in an arena. A brand new life flashed before my eyes, new opportunities. A life I would create myself. I could study Russian literature, business management, graphic design, philosophy, computer science, Italian Renaissance architecture—Ha! Whatever I damn well pleased. I wanted to explore, that's what I wanted to do until I found what clicked with me. Did I want to be a lawyer? Maybe. Did I want to be a social worker? Maybe. Did I want to be a magazine editor? A zoologist? Ooooh yeah, maybe.

I closed my eyes, my lips trembling, sinking into the chair my mother had left pulled from the table. My pulse roared in my ears, and I squashed the paperwork against my chest. All my hard work had paid off. All my dreaming of something else, somewhere else, was about to be fulfilled. I loved Meager, I did. It was home, but it was a blip on the map of the world I'd heard and studied so much about. A world I wanted to be a part of. I wanted to walk new roads and make new dreams, taste new flavors. Now I finally would.

I had to call Ruby.

Shooting up, I darted to the phone on the wall, dialing the number to the restaurant where Ruby used to be a waitress and was now the hostess. She got to dress up nicely and seat businessmen for their martini lunches. Since she'd gotten the job, she'd snagged the attention of a number of out of town businessmen. Married men.

"Eww," I'd said.

"Eww, huh?" Ruby pulled me into her room and closed the door behind us. "You know where I was last night?"

"No. Where?" I feigned indifference with a twist of my mouth and my arms crossing over my chest.

"At that new fancy casino in Deadwood with Mr. Eww. Amazing dinner, a bottle of pricey white wine, a couple of rounds of blackjack where there were cocktails, and I got to bet some of *his* money, and I won, thank you very fucking much. Then we went back to his hotel room—oh no, sorry, I mean, his hotel *suite*—jacuzzi, champagne, the whole deal. And it was fan-freaking-tastic. He was something. He had moves, and his dick was fucking huge."

"Rubeeeee!" My face scrunched.

"One day, Grace. One day you'll know what that means. Of course, it's only a good thing if the guy knows how to use his—"

"Stop!" I laughed loudly.

"Trust me, one day when you're not a virgin anymore, and you see your first big dick, you will think of me and mentally high-five me."

Since she'd got out of high school, Ruby only gave two cents about older men—meaning over twenty-five. Her junior and senior years, Ruby had dated Deke Hildebrand, Marshall's older brother. She really liked him. A lot. He was her first love, and they'd had sex (but he wasn't her first.) But after they'd graduated and had a super amazing summer together, he broke up with her the day before he left for Stanford. Ruby was shocked. Deke was unruffled, his parents relieved.

Ruby had been very upset, but she'd masked those emotions with bitter anger, picked herself up, and moved the hell along. She'd wasted no time in finding herself new boys to play with. First up was Deke's best friend, Tim Squiers, who stayed in Meager to work at his dad's store in Rapid. After Ruby got the initial shock out of her system with Tim, she dumped him, and thereafter, only played with *men*.

Males of all ages had always paid attention to Ruby. She had an athletic body, boobs, long legs and long blonde hair, big hazel eyes like mine, and a wicked grin to go with them. She was a California girl in the middle of South Dakota. Of course they salivated over her.

But it wasn't only her looks that attracted them. It was her fierce and fearless personality. She was a dare, but she was the one daring them, she was the one calling the shots. I don't know if they realized it, but they went for it, they really liked it.

I liked the way she called the shots, too.

I dialed the restaurant. "Hello, may I please speak to Ruby Hastings?"

Ruby got on the phone. "This is Ruby."

"Hey, Rube, it's me."

"What is it?" her voice sparked up. "You okay? You sound—"

"No, no, I'm not okay."

"What? Why? What's going on?"

"I got in to Denver."

"You what?"

"I got in. I got accepted to the University of Denver!"

"Grace!"

"I just got home from school and found the letter, I opened it—and, yeah … Can you believe it?"

"Yes. Yes, I can believe it," she said. "Don't you?"

My fingers tightened their grip on the phone. "Yes. Yes!"

"I'm so proud of you, honey. So proud of you. Did you tell Mom? Is she home?"

"No, she's not home, I don't know where she is. I wanted

to tell you first. I think I'm going to surprise Mom and Dad with it, so don't say anything yet. Okay?"

"Okay. I love you, Gracie," Ruby whispered hoarsely, and a warmth flared through my heart. She hadn't said those words in a long time, even though I knew they were true. "You deserve this. I'm real happy for you. This is going to be so amazing."

"I know it will. I'm going to call Tania, let her know."

"Okay. See you later."

"Rube?"

"Yeah?"

"Love you, too."

Chapter Six

"THANK God for your grilled cheeses, seriously." Tania twirled a thin, long strand of melted Swiss cheese around her finger, sucking it clean. She pushed her empty dish away on the counter of Drake's Cafe.

"How many of those do you eat? One a day?" I asked, slurping on the last of my iced tea.

"Pretty much. They're necessary to my life."

I made a face. "Swiss on whole wheat…"

"Don't make faces at my grilled cheese," said Tania.

"I prefer the classic American on white."

"You need to broaden your horizons, girl," Tania said, wiping at her fingers with her napkin.

"I'm good, thanks," I replied on a dry laugh.

"You guys need anything else? I'm taking off, so I need to close your bill, if you're ready, that is," said Erica, taking away Tania's empty dish and stashing it under the counter.

"No, we're good," said Tania as we both took out our money to pay. "Where are you off to?"

"Marshall's coming over so we can study Biology together."

"Biology, huh?" I let out a laugh.

"Those AP bio tests are no joke," said Erica, the lines of her face drawn.

"And your mom and dad? Are they going to be home, Miss Erica?"

"No, Miss Tania." Erica pursed her lips, her cheeks reddening. I sometimes forgot that most people didn't like talking the way Tania and I did. Erica wasn't as raw and twisted as we were. Well, we weren't so raw and twisted but blatant.

"Oooooo," Tania and I intoned together, twisting on our bar stools at the counter like little kids entertaining themselves.

"You guys, stop." Erica rolled her eyes, her lips pressing together as she took our money.

Tania leaned over the counter closer to Erica. "You better make sure you have your good bra and panties on. You know, to study properly."

"To get the most out of biology," I added.

"For Pete's sake, we really are going to study!" Erica slid us our change. "We have that midterm coming up, and…" Her fingers twisted in the towel on the counter. "That is a good idea, though."

"Hmm." Tania tilted her head in agreement. "You never know. Be prepared. That's all we're saying."

"Hey, hey, girls."

Tania and I swiveled on our counter stools at the sound of that booming voice. Marshall stood before us in all his hunky glory along with his best friend, Larry.

"Hey!" Erica's face softened, then tensed immediately. "What are you doing here? I thought you were going to come over to my house at five?"

"Change of plans." He shrugged. "I'm going to be late."

"Oh," Erica said, her voice dropping into Forlornville.

"Me and Larry got to take care of some stuff for the party."

"Party?" asked Erica.

"I just found out my parents and grandparents are going on their annual vacation to Florida early this year, so me and my brothers and cousins are getting our shit together now for the annual kegger at the ranch for this weekend."

"Wow. This weekend?" said Erica.

"Yep. Y'all better be there." He shot his all-American grin at each of us.

"Cool," Tania said.

"You bet," I added.

An enormous property, the Hildebrand ranch had been in their family for generations and kept getting bigger all the time. Recently, my mother had heard how the interior had been renovated and redecorated professionally. "I heard it looks like something out of *House Beautiful*," she'd said. "Can you imagine?"

We lived in Dad's mother's house, it was small and had only one bathroom. A lot of the furniture was from Grandma and Grandpa's day as well. My mother recently got a new oven, which was a huge win since Dad hated spending money. The dishwasher had taken him almost a year to replace, but an oven was kinda necessary in a more immediate way, and Mom had insisted.

"Larry and I got some stuff to take care of for the party, but I'll be there," Marshall said. "Half an hour late or so, okay?"

"Okay." Erica brightened up.

Chuckling, Marshall leaned over the counter, his now longer, off-season hair in his eyes, and planted a kiss on Erica's lips. She blushed, blinked, her shoulders relaxing as he pulled away.

Sigh.

They'd been dating steadily since Homecoming. Erica always seemed over the moon happy. Tania and I didn't really hang out with her. She was a cheerleader dating the school quarterback, and their social circles were beyond mine and

Tania's. We were somewhere in between the celebrity jocks and the rock slackers who wore black, chains and skulls, lots of eyeliner and dark nail polish, and smoked cigarettes.

"Later, ladies!" said Marshall on his way out of Drake's.

The three of us stared after them. Larry turned around and forming his fingers into a V and placing them against his mouth, he stuck out his tongue and flapped it lewdly at Erica as he moved out the door.

What the?

"What the hell was that?" asked Tania.

Erica went white.

"Erica?" I touched her hand on the counter. "You okay?"

"Oh my God," she said, her voice low.

"What is it? What the hell was Larry doing that for? And at you?" Tania said.

"I guess Marshall told him. I thought … gosh…" She pressed her lips together.

I glanced at Tania. "Told him what?"

"That we did *that*," Erica breathed.

"Ohhhhh," said Tania. "That Marshall went down on y…"

"Oohhh," I said, my foot kicking Tania's under the counter to shut her up.

"How was it?" asked Tania.

"Tan!"

Erica's face reddened. She blinked back the wetness gathering in her eyes. "I-I thought it was something special. We've been taking it slow, and this was an exciting step. For me, at least."

"Hey, Larry's an idiot. He's always been a clown. Remember freshman year when he mooned Mr. Reynolds? I mean, who moons the principal the first day of high school, right? He got detention for a month, his parents were so embarrassed. Then he teased that French exchange student and made her cry, remember that? That was bad. He has no filter, and he's kind of a bully. I'm sure Marshall would be real pissed if he knew that he did that. Marshall's not a jerk like Larry." I took in a breath. Did I convince her?

"I better go," Erica murmured, taking off her apron. She headed into the back of the coffee shop.

"Yikes," said Tania. "But hey, lucky Erica."

The buzz around school all week was the keg party. The Hildy ranch keg party was something of a legend in Meager. Even when Ruby and I were in junior high, the party at that ranch was a *thing*. People who had graduated would come to this party, it was that cool. Ruby and her girlfriends were planning on being there. I wondered if Deke would be there too. I sorta hoped he wouldn't.

Whatever. The social event of the season was upon us, and I was psyched.

Chapter Seven

ON THE NIGHT of the party, Tania brought a small duffel bag over to my house, and we spent a couple of hours trying to decide what to wear. She borrowed a pair of my dangly silver earrings to go with her black jeans and flowy blouse that she tied in a knot at her waist.

I was in my new, tight, pale blue jeans along with my old cowboy boots, a lowish cut burgundy T-shirt with a cool metallic copper and blue graphic on it, and my big gold-colored hoop earrings that I'd found at a vintage store in Rapid on a trip with Ruby.

"You look cute," said Tania from my bed, where she'd thrown herself in a fit of fashion exhaustion, heaps and piles of our clothes, shoes, boots lay around us on the floor of my room. "Those hoops look good on you."

I clomped over the piles to get to my full-length mirror. "Thanks." I smoothed the edges of my tee.

Tania raised herself up off my bed and popped opened the can of hair mousse she'd brought. "Let's do this." She applied the mousse to her hair, and I blew it out for her, getting her glossy black waves under control but with some volume. She applied mousse to my hair and worked on my unruly locks with the blowdryer.

We got our makeup on. I rarely wore base, but I figured tonight was a special occasion, so I splotched on the liquid foundation Tania had made me buy a while back, along with my favorite plummy blush and a soft brown eyeshadow I liked. I put more on than usual with a little shimmery brown eyeliner pencil Tania had. "Did I overdo it? Should I blend it more or take it off?" I reached for a cotton swab.

"You never overdo it. Are you kidding me? You look amazing," Ruby's voice came from my open doorway.

I grinned. "Thanks."

"We ready to roll?" My sister, in all her unfussy sexiness, stood in my doorway, her car keys dangling from her fingers. Messy, long, blonde hair that looked like she'd just woken up and had gotten "some," smudged mascara and black eyeliner pencil, and dark wine-colored gloss on her full lips. She wore ripped jeans with a new pair of cowboy boots, along with a tight Guns N' Roses concert T-shirt which she had cut open at the collar, her black lacy bra peeking out from underneath, and a choker at her throat. A big turquoise and silver ring stood out on her index finger, which I always thought was terrific. One good quality bold piece, not a hundred junky things hanging from her ears and fingers and neck. It made a statement. I liked that.

"Yep, we're ready." Tania fluffed out her hair for the millionth time. She wore a super dark red lipstick and black liquid eyeliner. Kinda vampy, but it looked good with her pale skin and big dark eyes.

I grabbed all our crap from the floor and dumped it on my bed into two piles, smushing them down so it didn't look like too much of a disaster. I didn't want to hear it from Mom later when Tania and I came home. Tania was spending the night, which was great.

"Where do you think you're going?" Mom's waspish voice

seared through my stomach. She stood there with a cigarette in her hand, her eyes lasering over Ruby, then me.

Ruby shot me her famed "I got this" look. *Oh no.* "We're going to a party."

"A high school party?" Mom gestured at Tania and me with her cigarette. "What the hell business do you have going to a high school party?"

This was that part of the recipe where I watched for signs of the first boil. I got in between them. Time to lower the heat on the pot. "Everyone's going, Ma," I kept my voice soft. *Defuse. Defuse.* "It's at the Hildebrand ranch. It's like a spring reunion every year."

"Right." Mom slanted her head at Ruby, a sardonic look souring her face. "You going to find Deke, aren't you? Show him what he's missing?"

"I don't give a crap about Deke," came Ruby's monotone reply.

"Right, right, 'course not." Mom's voice rose in that way I knew so well. My insides cramped with the needles and barbs entrenched in that voice. It was a bitter poison building.

Ruby said, "He can go fuck himself for all I care."

"Hey! What's going on over there?" Dad's voice rose from the other room, and my eyes widened.

"You're going to go over there and strut your stuff all over the place and make him notice you." Mom was on a roll.

Ruby's face remained unruffled. "You got that wrong, Janet. I don't have to *make* anybody notice me."

Motherfudgemycake.

"You two at it again? Cut the crap already," Dad's voice boomed over the television. "One night I'm home…"

Mom leaned into Ruby, and Ruby didn't flinch, but I did. "He doesn't get it, but I do," Mom's voice seethed, her lips twisting. "I would've thought that by now, you'd have better things to do on a Saturday night than chauffeur your little sister to her high school party."

"All Ruby's friends are going to be there, Mom. It's like a reunion party every year. It's spring break, you know?" My face heated, and I shot Tania a glance, my teeth scraping my bottom lip. "Sorry," I mouthed to her, and she shook her head once to show me "no biggie." Yeah, no biggie because Tania had witnessed a gazillion confrontations just like this between Ruby and Mom for years, all of them sour and pointless. But Dad was home today, and I didn't want this to get any worse now that he was here, because once he joined in…

The day had skimmed along just fine up until this very moment. We'd even managed an uneventful dinner, thanks to Tania being present. Dad had extended my curfew to midnight from 11:30.

Ruby only flicked her keychain in response. She really didn't care what mom said or didn't say. Her jaw tensed. She was waiting for the inevitable tumble of curses and name-calling, but the words didn't come today. Dad was home, and Mom was trying to ring in her temper.

Mom took in a deep breath, pressing her lips together, and they paled under the pressure. She scanned each of us intently, her harsh gaze lingering on Tania. "You trying to look like Madonna?"

Tania shifted her weight, a hand smoothing through her hair. "No, Mom!" I said. "We put on more eyeliner than usual and did our hair and—"

"I know what goes on at those parties," Mom said.

"You do, huh?" Ruby pushed back from the doorway, hands on her hips.

"I was in high school once, too, you know. Don't you dare get behind that wheel drunk. Don't you dare."

"I won't," Ruby said.

"Those One-Eyed Jacks going to be there? That why you going?" Mom's voice sharpened again, slicing right through my insides even though it was directed at Ruby.

"What would those guys want with a crowd of high

schoolers?" I said. "They have much more exciting ways to party than—"

"They certainly do," said Ruby, a grin warming her face.

Fuuuuuuuckkkkkkk. My stomach plummeted into a dark abyss under a two-ton slab of cement. *Why, Ruby? Whyyyyyy?*

Mom's eyes steamed, her mouth falling open. "You little tramp," her voice seethed.

Tania darted forward. "Mrs. Hastings, it's Saturday night, and the Jacks will be at the Tingle, right?"

"Exactly," I said, the tone of my voice unmistakably sparkly to dissipate the venomous fog in the hallway. "They're not going to waste their time at some high school party."

The Tingle was Meager's very own strip club on the edge of town that the One-Eyed Jacks owned. Lots of bikes and cars and trucks from different states were always parked there, especially on the weekends. Lots of men. Lots.

My mom shook her head, a hand cupping my chin. "Be careful, honey. You stay away from those bikers. Boys like that are nothing but trouble for girls like you."

"Don't worry, Mom." I planted a quick kiss on her cheek. She'd been drinking wine since before dinner, and the smell of the alcohol mixed with the cigarette smoke clung to her hair and clothes. She retreated, ambling down the hall toward the bathroom, a hand trailing the wall.

Ruby stared after her. "Let's get the hell out of here already."

In the living room, I laid a hand on my dad's shoulder. "We're off, Dad. Bye."

His eyes darted up at me from the TV screen. "Don't be late." He returned his attention to the game.

"We won't," I said.

"Bye, Mr. Hastings." Tania shot out the door. I stifled a laugh. She wanted to be polite but didn't want Dad to see her Madonna look.

Bugs and moths fought for the glowy real estate around

our yellow front door light. I hopped down the steps to Ruby's Grand Prix. Tania had already scrambled into the back seat. I slid in, slamming the door.

Ruby started her car, and it rumbled. I switched the radio on loud and Neneh Cherry got her buffalo stance on as we pulled out of the driveway, Tania singing along in the back seat.

Leaning back, I let out a long breath, my body sliding down the vinyl seat. *Finally.*

Chapter Eight

"HOLY CRAP," I murmured.

"Wow." Tania stumbled on the rocky earth.

"Catch you later," said Ruby, striding down the long hill to where a crowd swarmed.

It was almost ten o'clock, a bit past early for this kind of party, and yet there were a ton of people. The party wilded on in a vast, rocky, brush-filled valley at the sloping base of the house on the hill. The ranch house was lined by an outgrowth of rock and evergreens that guarded it like castle walls. A once traditional wood ranch house, now it was a sleek contemporary combination of wood and glass details with a new extension towering from the center.

Whoa. Mom was right. It was from a magazine. Dramatically lit by spotlights, the house stood vainly above and beyond us all, protected by a wall of tall trees, perfectly trimmed brush, and an iron gate to rival any Beverly Hills mansion I'd ever seen on TV.

The music blared loudly, and people were crowded around the two big kegs. Tania and I got into a line where we recognized a couple of friends from our history class.

"This is insane, y'all!"

"I'll say!" Tania shouted back.

Pickup trucks, bikes, cars were parked haphazardly everywhere. Several huge speakers were propped up on tables. People were dancing, laughing, all of them holding bottles of liquor or red plastic cups presumably filled with beer. A bonfire was to our right with another crowd around it. It was a pep rally of our own making. The night was *ours*.

We danced to *Funky Cold Medina*, laughing and tripping over ourselves. It was good to laugh, to laugh loud. To yell. We filled up on beer, and I took a big swallow of the brew. The thin, hoppy, slightly sour taste was nothing less than sheer awful and sheer perfection at that moment, and I gulped it down. The buzz zinged through me, and I relished it.

The flames of the bonfire licked and crackled in the night air. The flames danced wildly, their orange-red-gold glow over my skin, and their heat on my face filled me with a fervor of my own. Excitement and possibility, a touch of the unknown that lay before us. I took in a deep breath. The resiny pine in the air mixed with the roasting wood of the bonfire. We were living the life, at least for tonight. For now.

The pounding music had me not wanting to stop moving to its beat, so I didn't. Was it adrenaline? The beer? Catching Trent Evans's, the cute basketball player from English, appreciative grin as I bumped hips with Tania? And then he came over and grabbed my hand and danced with me? Yes, yes, yesssss.

We'd be graduating soon. The world was our apple, and we were ready to take our bite. Bite big. But until then, we were free of responsibilities—plain free.

The sky was clear tonight, and the stars ... millions of stars speckled the endless black velvet sky over us. We were in a special place, far away, tucked away, and blown open. No parents, no teachers, only us, us tonight.

Wiping beer from my mouth with the back of my hand, I scanned the party for my sister. I'd noticed her earlier dancing up a storm with a few of her friends. In the distance, I finally found the long blonde hair, the attitude etched on her face. Couldn't miss her friend Keith's hair—bright pink, and Katie had a streak of bright blue in hers.

Keith had been in the closet through high school, but once he'd graduated, he left Meager behind and finally came out. Life at Meager High had been pretty shitty for him. I remember Ruby telling me how he'd get teased for his fey mannerisms by the macho dudes in class, how they'd bully him mercilessly in gym. It would make Ruby so mad. She and Katie would always come to his defense in their own special ways, mostly by sliming the offenders' lockers, slashing the tires on their fancy jeeps and sports cars. Ruby had gotten suspended from school for a couple days on that charge. They were Marshall's fancy tires on his new Firebird, after all.

I admired Keith for breaking out and doing his thing, living his truth. Would I have the guts to do that one day? Whatever my truth was, of course. Now Keith was happy and making money, doing what he wanted far away from here, so ha-ha on those jerks, who were still living off Mommy and Daddy's dime, following the parent playbook. But here, now at this party, they were the kings, weren't they, and they were holding onto their kingdom for as long as they could. Senior year would soon be over.

"Hey, look who's here."

I pivoted at the snarling voice flaring behind me. Icy cold prickles raced up the back of my neck. Mike stood before me, sucking down a full cup of beer. His usually pale cheeks were red. He swiped at the froth on his lips.

"Hi."

"How you doing, Grace?"

"Fine."

"Right." He laughed, a low, lazy laugh, as he staggered toward me, a hand tugging on my shirt. "Nice shirt." His eyes glued to my chest. "I remember those boobs."

"Mike!" I stepped back from him, stumbling on the uneven, rocky ground. "Where's Michelle?"

Mike and Michelle Grant, the captain of the softball team, had started dating a few months ago. We'd even voted them "Cutest Senior Class Couple" for the yearbook.

He waved his cup in the air, and beer sloshed out. "She's here."

"Good. Why don't you go find her?" *Whoa, I can't believe I just said that.* With a new surge of energy, I spun, turning my back on him and darted into the flow of people, my pulse pounding with my every step.

Good.

For.

Me.

I spotted Katie on the opposite end of the valley from where I was. She was talking with three guys by a small fire in a metal bin. They didn't look familiar to me. They weren't from school. The one tall guy with a braid passed her a bottle, and she took a swig. All three guys were wearing the same leather vests with a fierce skull embroidered on the back. The One-Eyed Jacks were here.

A few guys approached them, and they spoke, exchanged things, hands tucked in pockets, heads nodding, grins all around. Oh man, they were selling drugs, weren't they?

"The Jacks are here?" came Tania's voice over my shoulder. She let out a cackle.

"Only three of them, though. Geez, after all that with my mother…" I laughed. "Can you believe it?"

"Well, Marshall and his brothers obviously want them here. I'll bet they buy from them and invited them tonight. They give me the creeps," said Tania.

"Why?"

"You hear all sorts of stories about their parties. My uncle says they do loads of illegal shit to make money. They're so arrogant, like nothing can touch them. Like they don't care about rules or—"

I laughed out loud, spilling my beer. "Well, that's the whole point of being a biker, isn't it?"

"Right, I guess." Tania laughed too.

"Maybe they give you the creeps because they fill you with a sense of the forbidden, and that actually excites you…"

"Shut up! Have you been reading your mother's sex-filled Harlequins again?"

I laughed. "No, no, no. Actually, I read "Nine and a Half Weeks." Holy shit, that was way different from the movie … crazy…"

"Really? I want to read it."

"I'll give it to you tonight," I said as I scanned the crowd for Ruby once more.

She was talking to Mike. Weird. She didn't seem happy with whatever Mike was rambling on about. Mike stood with Tim Squiers, Ruby's ex-friend with benefits. *Oh, great.* In fact, Mike seemed to be *rat tat tatting* words at Ruby, trying to make some sort of point, his body juggling forward, pointed finger in her face. Tim, with an arm on Mike, pulled him back up and away.

Mike was drunk, and Ruby was the ice queen putting up with the rabble. Tim seemed sober enough because he was eating Ruby up with his long, cold stare, a stare that traveled up and down her body, up and down. Keith came up behind Ruby, and Mike went off on him. A few more football players showed up at Mike's side. I recognized Larry and Manny.

"Uh-oh." Tania tugged on my shirt.

"What?"

"Is that Marshall?"

"Where?"

"There."

"Ooooh."

Marshall was wrapped around a girl who wasn't Erica. She had her hands under his shirt, and his hands squeezed her ass. She was pretty drunk and was much shorter than him, her head lolling back as she spoke to him, laughing, her hands roving, her body smashed up against his. And he wasn't pulling her off of him. He was lapping up whatever she was saying and enjoying her curves.

Having a crush on Hildebrand was a right of passage at Meager High. We all knew that, and we all went through it at some point, but only a tiny fraction got a chance to get up close. She was what I imagined a rock and roll groupie to be like. But man, how could he, and in public? He must be high with whatever the Jacks were selling.

"Fuck! Are you shitting me?" A roar rose up in the throng by the kegs. More shouts, hoots. Boos. "Oh, man! Someone broke the tap on the other keg."

"No way!"

Empty cups went flying. "How can there not be any more beer?" People shouted. "No more beer!" "Are you fucking kidding me?" Angry voices, hoots rumbled through the night air, clashing with the music. Marshall peeled himself off the girl and went running. The speakers tumbled over like Lego towers, and Eddie Vedder's voice jagged off into the night.

"Shit, maybe we should get out of here. Let's find Ruby," Tania muttered. We stood to the side, our beer gone, our adrenaline morphing into another type of adrenaline surge. Not the good kind we'd been feasting on all night.

Tania and I both rushed forward through the crowd, but a wave of people pushed us back. "What's going on?" I shouted, struggling, pushing.

"A fight broke out!"

"Fight!" came more shouting, pushing, and shoving. "Fight, y'all!"

The sharp point of a dagger tracked up my spine, searing me, gashing me. Something was wrong. I didn't see Ruby anywhere. I couldn't see, the surge of humans making it impossible. My chest constricted painfully as Tania tugged on my sleeve. "Let's get out of this crowd."

We tracked up the slope, but all the while, my insides plummeted. Something was wrong. I knew it. An eerie chill clamped at my squirming insides. We were moving in the wrong direction, and with every step up, that clamping twisted more, tightened more.

Roaring laughter rose from a cluster of football players at the base of the hill, and I jumped around. It was a different kind of laugh. Not a wide relaxed roll, but something stiffer, darker. Expectant.

"Let her go, let her go, you fucks!" Keith's voice screeched, and my heart stopped. My eyes pinned on Keith being held by two guys. He twisted in their hold. One of the guys—Manny—punched Keith in the gut, and he fell over.

"No!" Ruby howled, and my heart squeezed in two.

Tania and I ran, pushing through a group of people who were checking out the rumbling crowd below.

"Oh shit…" someone said.

"Is that Ruby Hastings?" another voice filled my ear as I pushed through the crowd.

"That's Ruby…"

Tim Squiers held Ruby by her arm, yelling at her, and she whipped around and punched him. His eyes widened, his chest puffed up, and he grabbed her face, her waist, yanking her hard. She laughed, her bitter, sharp fuck-you-you-fucking-loser laugh.

Tim smacked her, and Ruby's head jerked to the side with the force of his slap, her hair flying.

"Oh my God!" Tania gasped.

All at once, Ruby went flying—hair, her hands. Her legs kicked up, and my heart jumped up my throat and stuck there. Tim and Manny had grabbed her, hoisting her up like a trophy of war.

I froze. The scene blurred in my vision. Ruby's scream

filled the valley. A scream that ripped right through me. In her anger, I heard her fear. Ruby was scared.

My sister was never scared.

The footballers' voices rose in a chant "Yes! Yes! Yes! Yes!" Mike and Tim led the charge as Ruby kicked, punched, cursed. Keith yelled. The footballers laughed, their eyes hard, full of purpose as they hauled her up higher and out of the crowd.

"What, where are they—what the—" a girl in front of me stuttered.

My heart pounded wildly, kickstarting my blood, my senses, my brain as voices around me rang out.

"Are they gonna—"

"Oh, man! No way!"

I struggled for air as my brain zipped through the possibilities. One more harrowing than the next. There was no sense to be made. There was only a mob grinding together, a mob shouting together. Urging, craving, freaking.

Do it! do it! All right! All right!

No.

There was no way. There was no time.

"Stop! Stop! What the fuck!" Tania shouted.

Shouting wouldn't help.

Running there wouldn't help.

No one was getting in their way, trying to stop them, because no one dared to. They were the kings, the kings. The world had flipped upside down.

I had to do something to save Ruby. There had to be something. There was. One thing. One way. *If they're still here … please still be here.*

I swung, shoving through the rubbernecking assholes standing there gawking, ogling.

"Grace! Grace, wait! Where are you going?" Tania came up behind me, her hand tugging on the ends of my hair as I charged forward. I sucked in the sting of pain.

Yes. There they were. Where I'd last seen them.

The One-Eyed Jacks.

Men. Tall men. Hardened men. Somewhat bearded, long hair, messy hair, big leather jackets, chrome and metal bikes. Loud, cocky. Flipping the bird at the world. Everyone always telling me to stay away from them. The Jacks had been built up in my head as some sort of dark, dangerous, mysterious, bad…

I ran.

"Grace! Come back here! Grace—don't you dare!" Tania's words skipped off my back falling onto the rocks and dry earth behind me.

I dare. I dare.

Chapter Nine

I SKIDDED in front of them, kicking up dirt and dust, wiping my hair back from my face as I formed words. "Hey, excuse me, guys, can you help me?" My voice was louder than I expected, stronger. But that was good. I swallowed hard, my face burning as the three of them stared at me. One with suspicion, the other dark amusement, the third eyed me as he gulped from his whiskey bottle. Was I being impertinent? Was I not going to be taken seriously because I was just some girl?

"Those jerks have my sister!" My arm slashed in the air toward the party. The lines of their faces hardened. I had their attention. "He's slapping her around, and all his friends are laughing. They're gonna take turns with her. You've got to help me. Please!"

A young, attractive biker with hair almost touching his shoulders jumped down in front of me, a cigarette dangling from his mouth. "Is that what all that ruckus is about?" He wore a leather jacket over his colors, so I couldn't see his patches. He came close to me, his big brown eyes I could swim in frowned at me. "They got your sister?" he asked, his voice lowering.

I opened my mouth, no sound came out, no—

57

"Motherfucking football assholes!" hissed the taller one, tossing his liquor bottle to the ground. He hopped down from his perch, his long, braided hair hopping on his back. Rubbing his hands together, he let out a hard laugh. The name "Jump" was patched on his leather vest. "This party was a fucking bore and a half until now. Time to kick some school-boy ass." His warm fingers tweaked my chin. "We got this, little girl."

We got this.

YES! My pulse pounded in a triumphant gallop. They didn't even know me, but they were willing to help me. The three of them brushed past me. A force of vengeance, aggression in motion marched through the crowd, and my heart thudded. This wouldn't be a straightforward rescue and retrieval. Had I lit some kind of match between the town and the One-Eyed Jacks now? What if they ...Oh, shit.

You're thinking too much, Hastings!

I stumbled down the hill after them, the sea of people having parted for the three Jacks charging toward the mayhem. The air thickened, a hush fell. Doom awaited.

By the kegs, which now were dented and rolling around the ground and being kicked, Tim, Mike, and two others had raised Ruby up in their arms, a chant of *"Do it! Do it!"* reverberating in the air. Cavemen and their prey. A pagan sacrifice to the gods of ego and lust. Ruby kicked, her body twisting in their hold, and shouted a string of curses, but it only made them laugh harder, chant louder, tug harder. They were high on the rush of their supreme power, and more and more of the crowd got high along with them, chanting with them, throbbing for blood along with them.

The three Jacks reamed through the crowd like freaking commandoes, and with a roar, they pounced on Tim and his friends. Ruby went flying, Keith jumping at her, pulling her away. Shouting and yelling filled the air. The boys were caught completely off guard. They scrambled on the ground, howled, they had no worthy comeback for the Jacks' tornado touch-down and assault.

The Jacks showed no hesitation. They found their targets and went to town. Relentless. Tim Squiers was a bleeding rag doll in Brown Eyes's clutches as the Jack pounded on him non-stop. He'd found the chief offender and was going to town on him.

The thin Jack got a punch dead in the face from Mike, but he seemed offended, not fazed. He immediately socked Mike in the jaw, bringing a knee to his gut, and Mike toppled over and got kicks and curses until he pled for mercy. Jump took on two footballers at once, and they both fell on top of each other. He howled like a bear in the woods. Then he turned and pummeled Tim. Fighting was obviously not merely some hobby or a sport to the Jacks. It was serious business. They loved it.

Good to know.

The crowd scattered like ants, stumbling and racing off from the explosive fist assault. The tough guys who'd been cheering each other on only moments ago, ultimate power in their hands, had been lain to waste in the dirt. Blood now stained their precious varsity letter jackets. A chorus of *"no, wait, please no"* twittered in the air. They were begging for mercy.

Fuck you.

"Hey! Stop! Stop! Enough! Get off him!" shouted Marshall, hands in the air. "Get the hell out of here, you lowlife fuckers!"

The Jacks stopped, but ignored Marshall, looking only to each other, and they receded. They were experienced. They stuck together. They had each others backs.

Pushing people out of the way, the brown-eyed Jack deliv-ered a shuddering Ruby straight into my arms. "There you go, little sister," he said, his eyes still smoldering with the glory of battle, eyes glued to mine.

Burning heat shuddered through me, flaring through my veins, and I blinked. "Oh my God, thank you. Thank you so much, thank you." I held onto a shaky Ruby.

The thin biker with the very long dark hair came up next to him, his vivid green eyes glimmering. The name "Boner" was on his leather jacket. "Hey, it was a good time." Boner winked at me, wiping the blood off his face.

"Glad we could help," the brown-eyed one said. "You keep out of trouble, you hear? And get her to do the same." He jerked his chin in my sister's direction.

"Yeah, I know. Thanks again."

His steady gaze remained on me, the heat of it burning through me like a mountain wildfire, combusting everything in its path. "I bet you don't get into much trouble though, do you?" he said, his voice deeper, lower.

I swallowed hard. "N-no, not really."

Big Brown Eyes tilted his head at me and grinned. A shiver snaked through my insides. The thrill of the unknown, of temptation, of something wicked perhaps. A *thrill*, not fear. That was new for me, and I didn't know what to do with it. I let that sensation sizzle and dissipate in the air between us. I wanted it gone, I wanted it back.

"Too bad." He lifted his chin. "See you." Big Brown Eyes and his brothers left us, tracking over to their Harleys. They revved up their bikes, and the grinding roar filled the night and vibrated in my insides.

Ruby and I stood there, our arms wrapped around each other, the two of us shivering, watching as they thundered off one by one. My eyes sank closed. They'd done it. I'd done it. Everything was going to be okay.

Well, for now.

"Hot damn," Ruby murmured.

"You okay?" I whispered in my sister's hair.

"Yeah. I'm okay." She turned in my arms. "How did they … they saw and came running—"

I grinned. "I asked."

"You asked?"

"Uh-huh."

"Jesus. She asked." She kissed the side of my head and gave me a squeeze.

"What the hell happened? I heard you yelling. I saw them lift you up. I was so scared. What the hell is their problem?"

"They're little boys with narrow, dented minds and tiny dicks, and they think the world is theirs. And anyone different is wrong."

"They were taking shots at Keith."

"Yeah, but your old boy toy Mike—"

"I saw him, what the hell—"

"He was drunk and touched me, tried to tell me that you wouldn't give him the time of day, wouldn't put out for him after he laid down the red carpet for you—"

"Red carpet? What the—"

"Yeah. So he thought we owed him, and I was a sure thing because he'd heard all about me. Goddamn Tim. He's still pissed at me for blowing him off. See what happens? You sleep with more than one guy, suddenly they *all* think you're a ho in a vending machine for them. Fuck that. Tim served a purpose. We had fun. Done. Some idiots can't handle that. They need to be the big man in the equation at all times. The bikers, though. You know what you're getting into with them. I like that."

"Rube!"

"I'm so glad you dropped Mike's ass when you did," she continued. "His ego couldn't handle it. That's a basic man problem, and don't you ever forget it. Learn to spot it."

I let out a huff of air. "He always seemed like the good guy of that whole crew. Boy, was I wrong."

"I'm glad you listened to your instinct."

"Me too." I was really glad I'd listened to my instinct

tonight by going to the Jacks for help. "I'm glad that Jack beat him up."

"That was amazing. The sight of Tim on the ground, wailing, begging for mercy, and Jump telling him NO and laughing. I will never forget that moment. Ever."

"Me neither."

Her lips pulled in, setting in a firm line. "It's over, and they got theirs. And I'll be getting mine."

"What does that mean?"

"Now I have an excuse to get over to the Jacks' clubhouse for their next party. I've been trying to get an in with them for a while now, and now I have one. I can go over there and thank Jump personally."

"Great. Can we go home now?" I said. The adrenaline rush was now dragging through me big time.

"Y'all okay?" Tania came up to us.

"Yep," I replied.

"You think the Hildies called the cops?" asked Tania.

"No way," said Ruby. "Too humiliating. And they don't want their precious party screwed with." Ruby clutched at her side with a grimace and a grunt.

I grabbed her bicep. "What is it?"

"I think I have to go to a doctor. I got kicked … I think it's a rib … fuck."

I nabbed her car keys from her pocket. "Let's get the hell out of here."

Chapter Ten

WHAT DO you mean someone grabbed you?" Dad asked Ruby, staring at the bruising, which had gotten uglier overnight.

Ruby held his stern gaze in the kitchen where I'd come in to make a cup of tea first thing in the morning. *Oh shit.* My fingers tightened over my tea bag.

"I asked you a question, Ruby Hastings. I expect an answer." But there was no reply from Ruby. Dad's sharp gaze drilled into me. "*You* want to answer my question? You got bruises on your arms too?"

"No—"

"No, you don't have bruises, or no, you don't want to answer my question?"

The last thing I wanted was a confrontation between Dad and Ruby. I'd woken up happy in the knowledge that Mom had gone to Pierre to visit her sister, our Aunt Lucy, who'd started chemotherapy this week, so she wouldn't be back for at least a week or so. We'd assumed Dad wouldn't be hanging around the house as usual. We were wrong. Thank God he hadn't noticed the bandage around Ruby's middle. Yet.

"No, I don't have bruises," I replied, my fingers crumpling the tea bag in my hand.

"Good. Ruby?"

Ruby held his gaze. "Because I got into an argument with some assholes at the party last night. They got mad and decided to show me who was boss."

"Is that it?"

"Not enough?"

"Oh, no, it's plenty. But I know there's more you're not telling me. There's always more with you."

Father and daughter engaged in one of their legendary staredowns, and my stomach knotted tighter to the tune of the big sunflower clock over the dinette table. That dull *click, click* shuddering the seconds, the moments, the…

"Rube—" I pleaded.

Ruby only shot me a dark look.

Dad stood tall, stiff. "Answer me, young lady."

She didn't answer him.

"Was it the Jacks?" he said. "I'm sure they were there. Don't you even try denying they were there."

"They were there," Ruby replied. "But it wasn't them."

"Oh, I knew it."

"It wasn't them!" I said.

"Then who? What happened, goddammit?"

"It was more than the one jerk," Ruby said.

"What—"

"But nothing happened!" I jumped in.

His eyes flared. "Nothing happened? Boys—more than one—grab your sister and give her bruises, and that's *nothing*?"

"I only meant—" I hopped up on my toes.

"Are you kidding me?" Dad's hard gaze darted between Ruby and me. "Did they threaten you not to tell anyone? Is that it?"

"No!"

"Then what?" Dad's voice boomed in the kitchen. "'Cause this is plenty wrong from where I'm standing right now!"

"It is wrong!" I stood between them. "That's why I asked the Jacks who were there for help, and they got her out."

Dad's eyebrows bunched.

"There were three One-Eyed Jacks there checking out the party, and Grace asked them for help," Ruby replied, her tone even.

Dad's wide eyes landed on me. "You asked, and they helped?"

"Yes. They heard the commotion, and when I told them what was going on and asked them if they could get Ruby safe, they ran down there right away. They got her free and …."

"And what?"

"Punched those assholes down to the ground, that's what," said Ruby, eyes gleaming.

"They brought Ruby to me, Dad. Said they were glad they could help and—"

"And then what?" he spit out.

"And then they took off on their bikes."

"They just took off?"

"Yes, sir," I said.

Dad sucked in air, his chest rising, his hands on his waist. "Do you know what could have happened to you, to both of you, if you hadn't asked them for help? If those Jacks hadn't been there?"

Ruby shifted her weight, her gaze falling to the ground. Dad grabbed her shoulders, shaking her, and she winced, his voice throttling through the kitchen, throttling my heart. "Do you know—" His holler caught in his throat. He was upset. He was worried.

Ruby's hand cuffed Dad's. "I know, Dad. I know."

He swallowed hard, that muscle along his jaw ticking. "How did it start?"

"They were saying mean crap to Keith, and I called them on it," Ruby said. "Then they ran out of beer, and I told them they couldn't even throw a good party. It was supposed to be a keg party, for Pete's sake—"

Dad's head fell forward for a moment. "Ruby—" He raised his head once more, a tight grin lacing his lips. "Who grabbed you? Who was it?"

"Dad—"

"Don't you defend him to me, girl."

"Tim Squiers."

His head slanted. "Didn't you go out with him a couple of summers ago?"

"How do you remember that?"

"Why did he—"

"He was being a jerk—"

"About Keith?"

"Not only. He tried to…"

An ominous noise growled in Dad's throat. He got what Ruby meant.

"Then Mike Dubransky was trash-talking about Grace and how she owed him, and so did I, so I told him where he could stick his sorry-ass di…"

My eyes widened, my heart thrashed against my chest.

Dad's face tightened. "Who. Else?"

Ruby rolled down the names for Dad. All five, all five who had hurled her up in their clutches, having their laugh, threatening her with their worst. The God-awful worst.

Dad shook his head at each name, and with every shake, disgust and anger smoldered on his face. "You and Grace grew up with these shits. I grew up with all their daddies. Motherfuckers—" He grabbed his corduroy jacket from a chair. "You stay here. Both of you! Do not move!" He tracked out of the house, the front door slamming behind him, his dark orange Jimmy roaring to life in the driveway.

I ran to the front window and pulled back the curtain as

the Jimmy screeched at the stop sign at the end of our block and careened from view. "Oh my God, where's he going? Do you think he's going to the police? Shit!"

"Who knows." Ruby slid on the table, her long legs dangling, her jaw stiff.

She didn't know what to think. Neither did I. I was glad Mom wasn't here. She would have frazzled into a hysteria, and it would only have made things worse than they already were. I was glad Dad knew. I was glad the Jacks had their way with those jerks. But now what? Dad going to the police would make things hell for me at school. Hell for Ruby wherever she went. Hell for the Jacks too. And hell for the Hildebrands. That party would never happen again.

I threw myself onto the sofa, burying my face in a pillow. "I really don't want to go to school on Monday."

"Sorry, Gracie."

I lifted my head up. "It wasn't your fault."

"They pissed me off, and I took the opportunity to let them have it. I couldn't let it go."

"They junk talk all the time, and we have to take it, but they can't handle a girl dishing it out. Screw them."

"Screw them." Ruby's lips turned up into a smile. "Don't ever forget this feeling, Gracie. Don't."

"I won't."

"No matter what happens with Dad, the police, the Hildebrands, Tim, Mike, and everyone—"

"What if the One-Eyed Jacks get mad at us, blame us for problems with the town?"

"I'll bet they'll love it, don't worry about them. Whatever happens today, you and me have to suck it up as usual. But we're right."

"We are right, Rube."

She slid off the table. "You hungry?"

"Are you cooking?"

"Want cheesy scrambled eggs and sausage? There's sausage, right?"

"There's always sausage and cheese in this house."

In the kitchen, I got out the eggs, American cheese, the frozen sausage Dad brought from Montana regularly, bread and butter. I sat on the table and drank from the carton of orange juice as Ruby cooked us one of her amazing breakfasts.

Of course, I'd have to clean up after, and Ruby always made a big mess no matter what she cooked, but that was totally fine. She was a good cook when she wanted to be.

———

WE'D EATEN in front of the television, then gotten into a food and brain daze over Saturday morning cartoons and the shopping channels. Ruby had fallen asleep, and I'd cleaned up the kitchen. The loud grind of the Jimmy in the driveway woke her up, and she popped up off the couch. It had been over two hours since Dad had left.

I shut off the television. "Dad?"

"I went to see the pride of Meager High—Tim, Mike … everyone's dads. I told them I wouldn't press charges against their sons for what they did and could have done to Ruby if they didn't press charges against the Jacks who beat-up their precious boys. That's one hell of a black eye and bruised jaw on Tim, by the way."

"Hmmm." Ruby grinned.

"And?" I asked.

"They agreed. They've all got college acceptances and family reputations to protect, you know."

I bit my lip.

He ripped off his jacket and threw it on the sofa. "Then I went to the Jacks' clubhouse—"

Ruby raised an eyebrow.

"You what?" I said.

"I went to the MC's clubhouse and thanked them. I shook hands with each and every member, looked them in the eye, and thanked them for standing up for you."

Ruby and I shared a quick glance.

"I told them about the deal I made with all the fathers, and they appreciated it. A show of respect and gratitude always gets appreciated if it's genuine."

"Holy shit," fell from my lips.

Ruby's head knocked back, and loud laughter poured out of her. Dad rolled his eyes at her. "What's so funny, Ruby?"

She fisted her hands and raised them high. "Outlaw justice has been served."

"Damn straight," said Dad. "Good enough for me. Better, in fact."

"I agree," said Ruby.

"Thanks, Dad." I hugged him, and he gave me a quick squeeze and headed into the kitchen toward the coffee maker. "So, what's their clubhouse like?" I asked.

Dad poured himself a cup of coffee. "They fixed up the old go-kart factory real nice. Good for them. They got a big repair shop up there for bikes and cars. They even told me to bring them the Jimmy for a tune-up. The muffler's gone to shit anyhow, so I just might."

"Nice," Ruby murmured.

"I'm paying, though," he said. "I don't want them thinking we owe them, you hear?" He shot Ruby a pointed look.

"Yep," she said on a smirk.

Oh geez. "You want something to eat, Dad? Eggs and—"

"That'd be real nice."

Ruby and I got busy in the kitchen.

I pressed my lips together, but inside I was grinning like a fool. Dad did all that for us? He talked down all those dads, who were probably itching to have an excuse to blast the MC.

They could have easily turned it around and made it look like the Jacks were the ones who'd caused the trouble. Who'd assaulted Ruby, even. Dad had stood up for what was right, for us, and served them and their sons with the brutal truth and made a deal. A deal! Then, topping it all off, he went to the Jacks and thanked the bikers personally for helping his daughters. My head spun.

Dad sipped on his coffee as he flipped through the newspaper. Maybe this was a turning point for all of us. Dad got involved, and there'd been no blaming, no crazy defensive arguing. Only Dad caring about how his daughter had been treated badly and could have been hurt worse. How those jerks were wrong and needed to be called out, no matter who they were. How the bikers he sometimes grumbled about had been standup guys and deserved a personal thank you and a save from a possible inflated attack against them.

I set the table for Dad, and as Ruby slid his eggs into a dish, I buttered his toast. "Here you go." I set the toast on the edge of his dish.

"Thanks, Gracie."

Everything was all right with the world in a way it hadn't been in a very long time.

And never would be again.

Chapter Eleven

MOM GOT the watered-down version of what had happened because we all knew she would go over to all the mothers of the football jerks and make a stink. As far as me, Ruby, and Dad were concerned, it was case closed. We left well enough alone.

My eighteenth birthday had finally arrived. Did I feel grown-up? I guess. I wasn't a kid anymore, right? Right. But the girl who looked back at me in the mirror still had those freckles, that brown hair, the easy grin, that fair-skinned face that blushed easy. I'd never win at poker. I tousled my hair and made a tough girl face. Yeah, yeah. I could be tough. I could be badass.

Dad and Mom gave me the pearl bracelet that had been Grandma's. That bracelet had been in my mother's family since the gold rush days. Ruby had gotten a used car for her eighteenth that she'd put money into as well. I would have liked a car too, but I was happy with the bracelet. It was a family heirloom that belonged to all the women in Mom's family. Mom was the eldest sister, and she'd gotten it from her mother, and so on. It was dainty and feminine. I could wear it if I ever got dressed up for something one day.

"You can wear it whenever you want, you know," I said to Ruby, who fingered the sleek pearls at my wrist.

"Here. Happy birthday, Gracie." She handed me a small box wrapped in ribbon. It was from our favorite vintage shop in Rapid.

I ripped it open. A silver peace sign necklace decorated with tiny crystals. The chain was very slight and short, so I knew it would lay perfectly at the base of my throat. "I love it! Thank you!" I grabbed Ruby in a tight hug, and she laughed. "Put it on me." I moved my hair out of the way, and Ruby fastened the chain around my neck.

I darted to the mirror by the front door. "So pretty. I love that it's retro and kind of boho."

"I knew you would."

Dad took us all out for a birthday dinner in Rapid to his favorite steakhouse. Things had been kind of quiet and easy-going around the house lately. There weren't fights and squawks between him and Mom, who seemed relaxed. Plus, she'd been made manager of the bowling alley where she worked and was happy with the upgrade. Maybe things were looking up.

"I have a surprise of my own tonight," I told my parents. Ruby grinned.

"You do?" Mom said, lifting her wine glass. "I love surprises!"

"I got into the University of Denver."

"You what?" said Mom.

"I found out a couple of weeks ago, but I wanted to surprise you with it tonight."

"Honey! I'm so proud of you!" Mom jumped up from her seat and hugged me.

Dad laid a hand on my shoulder and squeezed. "Good for you."

Ruby raised her glass. "Here's to Gracie and her new life. Buh-bye, Meager! Woo!"

"Oh, stop, you!" said Mom as we all clinked our glasses together.

We drank. We drank to my eighteenth birthday. We drank to good things happening for us. We drank to my future full of new horizons.

And that was the last good moment I remember before it all crashed and burned, and our lives were changed forever.

Changed?

No, no. Lame word.

Ripped the fuck apart.

____

Chapter Twelve

I HAD a date for the prom. Trent Evans, the basketball player I'd danced with at the keg party, asked me and I said yes. We'd gotten flirty since the party.

Trent and I were in a couple of classes together, and ended up being project partners in a Social Studies debate. We went out a couple of times. He was tall and had dark hair that flopped in his brown eyes. He was cute and funny and had a deep voice that set off sparks inside me. I liked him. And he was a good kisser.

Tania and I left chemistry together, Mike zoomed out in front of us to his girlfriend, Michelle, who always waited for him in the hallway. Mike slid his arm around her shoulder as they talked by his locker. He and I ignored each other entirely now, and I didn't feel one iota of guilt about it like I did before.

That was something.

"So tonight," said Tania. "Le prom at last."

"Prom!" I responded.

"Your parents are actually letting you stay out past midnight?"

"Dad's away and, luckily, Mom really likes Trent, so she

didn't give me a hassle about it. Plus, ever since I got into Denver, she's been all "Have fun!"

"Lucky for me, my mother is visiting an old friend of hers in Nebraska, and she's taking my little brother, the hellion, with her, which means, my sister will be out with her boyfriend all night, and I'll be at my house with mine." She waggled her eyebrows.

"Score," I said.

"Exactly."

Tania and her new boyfriend, Andy, had started having sex. Like twice. It happened in his basement, where he had his TV and video games set up. They could hear his parents watching television in the living room over their heads.

"Finally, alone and a bed," Tania's eyes flared as she slammed her locker. "I'm planning on a big, lonnnng evening."

"I'm afraid to ask."

She leaned into me as we walked toward math. "First off, I want him to go down on me already," she whispered.

"Well, you've done him the favor, it's about time," I said.

"Right? He keeps saying, 'what if my parents come downstairs?' Of course, me doing it to him isn't a problem, or us doing IT real quick on the couch, but no, him doing THAT on me is a whole other … you know what I mean." She blew out a huff of air. "So, I figured since we'll have my house to ourselves, meaning total privacy, plus an actual bed to stretch out in…"

"Yeah, sure." I tried to sound convincing.

They were always fooling around, and if Andy hadn't done it yet, I really didn't think he was going to now. Ruby had told me that some guys really like it, and some guys don't like it at all and always try to avoid it or plain refuse to do it. At prom, the pressure for Andy to perform would definitely be on, and Tania was setting the stage—literally, with her bed—

with high expectations. I had my fingers crossed that Tania was right, and Andy would go for it.

"Plus, when we do do it"—continued Tania in a low voice —"it's always really fast like we're hiding or on the run or something—I guess we are down in his basement. But I don't get much out of it. Frankly, for me, it's kind of awkward and uncomfortable."

"I'll bet. Have you told him that?"

"No. Not yet. But I figure if we're alone and have plenty of time to ourselves, he'll be relaxed and we can really get into it and enjoy it and … yeah." Her teeth scraped her lip as she adjusted her bag strap on her shoulder.

"Hmm…" My tone remained perky. I didn't know what to say. Man, sex was kind of complicated, wasn't it?

I spotted Miller walking up the opposite lane in the hall. A dark blue and purple swirling graphic blared from the paper cover of the book in his hand. I still noticed his covers. That one was new. Totally amazing. His shiny black hair swung as he loped down the hall, his dark eyes shuttered against the noise and the chaos of the hallway. A girl walked with him, clutching her books to her chest, talking excitedly. He'd gotten muscular over the school year, filled out, seemed taller, even. His dark-red, short-sleeved T-shirt hugged the curves and contours of his torso, and his chiseled, tanned arms were impressive.

His stern gaze snagged on mine, and the bleakness of those eyes seemed to lift for a moment. They gleamed at me, and my pulse skipped. "Hey," he said, the lines of his face softening.

"Hey," I returned on a grin, and his full lips seemed to tip up for a moment. His attention went to the girl at his side, and we moved past each other in the flow of hall traffic.

It's not like we knew each other or talked or anything, but ever since that time in the assembly back in September, we'd say hi to each other. Just hi or a look, a smile. With some people, you stopped doing that after a while, but he and I kept it up. I guess we were both polite types.

"Have you thought anymore about … you know…" Tania's elbow poked me back to reality.

"Huh? Oh."

Tania had been after me for weeks to give up my V-card on Prom night, but I wasn't super enthusiastic. I didn't want to "give it up." That phrase rubbed me the wrong way. And it wasn't some "card" either. It was a once in a lifetime thing that happened to a girl. Tania had told me about her first time doing it in the dark by the light of the television playing WWF, Hulk Hogan growling loudly and Andy doing it super quick, squashing her on the sofa, her jeans and panties at her ankles lest his parents came downstairs to check on them.

No thanks.

I didn't have stars in my eyes about having to be in love to have sex, but I wasn't interested in doing it to get it over with or something. I wanted my first time to be with someone I felt all warm and gooey over. That heart-pounding feeling I'd always read about in romance books. Seen in movies. Imagined for myself. I wanted that for my first time. I didn't feel any rush to do it, not like when I was dying to get my driver's license the second I'd turned sixteen.

Anyhow, Trent and I had only been seeing each other a few weeks, and I can't say I was head over heels in wow with him. We got along great, he was funny, protective, but I wasn't doodling his name all over my notebooks. And I felt that when we did fool around, it was more about him *doing*, rather than *us*. I was asking for too much, maybe.

For Tania, sex was this achievement she'd wanted to claim and master. For Ruby, sex was a fun, feel-good indulgence she gave herself. My life would certainly be easier if I had that what-the-hell bold and brazen attitude of hers. I thought too much, and I felt too much, or at least, I wanted to feel all that "too much." I couldn't shut that off. Was I supposed to shut it off?

Maybe my lukewarm reaction to the whole idea of doing it with Trent was telling me I didn't like him enough. I didn't want my first time to be simply an extension of fooling around. My timing was off, I guess. When the heck would my timing be right?

Chapter Thirteen

WE'D BEEN TO PROM, we'd eaten at the class breakfast afterward at Drake's where the King and Queen, Marshall and Erica, sat at a decorated table with their friends. And then everyone took off. Tania and Andy were all smiles, holding hands, glued to each other as we'd said goodbye on Clay Street by Andy's car.

"What are you two up to now?" Andy asked Trent. "'Cause nobody's home at Tania's casa. We got the whole place to ourselves. You should come over."

Tania's face fell.

"Um—" I started.

"Sounds great. Huh, Grace?" said Trent.

"Sure."

Andy gestured at his car. "I got plenty of booze in my trunk."

"All right!" Trent high-fived Andy.

"Sure. Come over." Tania grinned tightly.

At Tania's house, Andy and Trent poured whiskey into glasses that Tania and I used to drink our chocolate milk from when we were younger. Tania had put music on and lit one vanilla-scented candle. I knew she had an arsenal of candles waiting to be lit in her bedroom. We sat on the sofa and talked and drank. At least Tania pretended to drink. She didn't like whiskey much. I was kind of used to it because Mom and Dad were always drinking it around the house and I'd sip the leftovers.

Tania and Andy got giggly and handsy, and soon enough were fooling around on the couch. "Tonight was fun, huh?" Trent murmured against my throat, his lips brushing my skin. We kissed, our tongues tangling. His arms slid around me firmly, and he adjusted me closer against him on the sofa. "I was going to take you to the reservoir, a bunch of the guys from the team are heading there with tents and shit, but this is way better, huh? I hate fucking camping."

His firm, large hand traveled down my thigh and quickly found the hem of my long dress, yanking it up. "And anyhow, who wants to worry about bugs when you're…" His mouth crushed mine. My back stiffened, my hands clutched at his arms. Tania and Andy had disappeared.

Trent stroked my bare thigh up and down. His hand went to my chest and squeezed my one boob tightly. I grit my teeth. His fingers peeled back the top of my dress, and his wet tongue danced over my boob and found my nipple. A gasp escaped my lips.

"You like that, huh? Me too…" He chuckled as he palmed my breast right out of my dress, and clutching it tightly, suckled on me. My jaw tensed, my toes dug into the floor. His free hand was between my legs, his fingers digging into my panty.

"Trent—"

But Trent didn't hear me. Trent couldn't hear me. He was into getting himself some. I didn't want any though. I didn't want this.

I twisted slightly in his tight hold. I pushed against him. But Trent was a rock. A rock on a mission.

"Isn't this cool? We're here alone," Trent murmured

against my skin. "I was thinking….how about I go down on you—" he squeezed my crotch—"and then you go down on me, huh?" He let out another low chuckle and nibbled on my shoulder.

"Uhm…" I tugged at my strapless bra.

He pulled back, licking his lips, a hand squeezing my butt. "It'll be so good. So good…"

My heart banged in my chest. I could barely swallow past the uproar. I'd never done that before and I didn't want to start now. With him. Like this. "Trent, I don't think—"

"What?" Trent's head jerked back, his eyes narrowing. "What's wrong?"

My skin tightened. I was on the witness stand, all eyes on me. *No, Trent, I don't want to suck on your dick.* "I-I just want go home."

"Are you kidding?" His sharp tone pierced my veins with ice. He was angry.

"No, I'm not kidding."

He released me from his hold, pushing me like I disgusted him. "What the hell? Why not?" He dug a hand through his hair. "What's wrong with you?"

"Excuse me?"

"You had sex with Mike. So what's the big deal about giving me a—"

"What?"

"He said that…"

Oh my God!

"This is bullshit," Trent muttered. "Total bullshit. I thought that this summer…"

I sat up straight, adjusting my dress. "Can you take me home?" My voice was low, my body stiff. A rush of shame and anger twisted through me like an old steam locomotive that had hurtled off the tracks, tumbling and crashing. I headed for the front door.

"I don't believe this shit!" He shook his head, pressing his lips together, grabbing his jacket from the floor.

I went outside, sucking in the chilly night air, but my throat still burned. We got in his car, and he slammed his door shut and pulled out of Tania's driveway, the engine protesting under his heavy hand and jerky directives. I crossed my arms tightly, pressing myself against the seat the whole five and a half minutes it took to get to my house. He didn't pull up the driveway.

I got out of the car. There was nothing to say. I didn't want to say anything. My body shook as I tracked up the pathway to my front door. Trent sped off, and I peeled his pink corsage from my wrist, tore off the flowers.

The worn petals fluttered to the ground.

———

"HE ONLY LICKED ME TWICE. Maybe three times," Tania said over the phone the next afternoon.

"Whaaaaat?" Curled up with the phone on my bed, my fingers picked at a worn seam on my daisy quilt. "Are you kidding me?"

"I wish I was. He suddenly stopped and got a rubber on and climbed on top of me and started. I swear..."

"Did you say anything?"

"How could I? He was all, "Oh, Tania, I'm so hard, got to do it now,'" she said in a fake man voice. "And then bam, he was inside me, going to town."

Ouch.

"Well, at least it must have been better because you were alone and in a bed for a change?" *Miss Look on the Bright Side, here, at it again, trying her best.*

"That's the stupid part. No," Tania's voice clipped.

"No? What do you mean, no?"

"He just jackhammered away, holding my legs apart. I

mean, excuse me, sir, but hello, I'm here, and I'd like to have my good time too. I guess he thought I'd come already because I was moaning loud on licks one, two, and three, but that was because I was so excited and I wanted him to keep going. I really figured he'd be into it seeing me all into it, you know? But no."

"I'm so sorry."

Yeah, sex was complicated.

"At least I learned what *bad in bed* means. When the guy is only thinking of his own dick. Like he has to feed that beast pronto, and that's it. I still wasn't comfortable. He was holding me in a way that he could get the best access, but for me, it was awkward and…" She let out a groan. "Whatever. Isn't sex supposed to be more give and take sort of thing? Wanting to make each other come…"

"I think so," I replied.

"Anyhow, my sister ended up coming home early, and Andy took off. Oh well, maybe one day…" Her bitter voice trailed off into a hollow laugh.

"You will. We both will. We have our whole lives ahead of us for lots of amazing sex."

"That's right. Fingers crossed. So what happened with you and Trent?"

"We fooled around a little bit, then he took me home. He was pissed off that I didn't want to do more. He said Mike told him that we'd had sex. Can you believe that?"

"What an asshole! And yes, I do believe it. You think Mike's going to burst that ego bubble to his buds?"

"I guess not."

"Grace, get off the phone, please!" Mom's voice rose from the kitchen. She was irritated. *Now what?*

"Just a sec!" I yelled back. "Tania, my mom needs to use the phone. I'll call you later. You going out at all?"

"Heck no. Microwave popcorn and the VCR are calling my name tonight. Come over if you want."

"Sounds perfect. Bye." I clicked off the cordless phone, then scrambled off my bed and headed for the kitchen. "I'm off the phone, Mom." I stilled in my tracks.

She'd been crying. Her face pale, lips thin.

"Mom? Are you okay? What's going on?"

"Your dad. Your dad is missing."

Chapter Fourteen

"It's been over two weeks since he went on that job to Oregon. He should have been back the day before yesterday."

"You didn't say anything."

"I thought it was him being late. And anyway, with your prom and everything … and I haven't been feeling well, I lost track of time, and …"

"And you haven't heard from him?"

"No."

"Um, have you called the company?"

"That's what I wanted to do now."

She picked the old phone on the kitchen wall with the long, coiled cord, and dialed the trucking company Dad worked for. I leaned against the wall as she spoke to whomever.

"You're sure?" her voice was even. "Hmm. Okay. Thanks." She slowly returned the phone to its cradle.

"What? What did they say?"

"They said that he finished his route on time."

"That's it?"

"And that he's not on the schedule for another week."

"Oh. You mean, he's off this week?"

My mother brushed her hair back behind her ears. "I think we better start calling hospitals … I don't know…"

We called the police station, but there had been no traffic accidents. We called the hospitals in Rapid, a couple others off the route we knew Dad took to go west. Nothing. My heart thudded dully in my chest.

What was going on? Where was he?

"I don't understand." Mom slumped in her chair at the kitchen table, lighting her hundredth cigarette.

"I don't know, Mom. I'm going to call Ruby. Maybe she talked to him." *As if.* But you never knew. I headed into my room to use the cordless.

"What do you mean he's *missing*?" Ruby said over the phone. Her tone was laid back. She wasn't buying it.

"You haven't talked to him?"

"No."

Dizziness swirled slowly up through my neck, my head. An icy prickle needled over my clammy skin. "Can you come over, because …"

"I can't now. For God's sake, he'll turn up. He always does."

"Rube." My voice came out sharper, more demanding than I expected. "Please. We need you, dammit."

"Okay. I'm on my way."

Ruby came and made coffee. I put away the wine bottle my mother was close to finishing. Ruby made calls to a couple of Dad's trucking friends whose names and numbers we found in an old address book she found in his night table drawer. They hadn't spoken to him in weeks.

"He's a shit," said Ruby as we made spaghetti and meat sauce for dinner while Mom parked herself in front of Wheel of Fortune with a glass of wine. "I'll bet he's got a girlfriend and he took her to Florida and they're drinking Mai Tai's while we're here—"

"Shut up, that's not helping."

"We should check his bank account. That would fucking help."

My stomach tightened into its hundredth twisty knot of the evening. He couldn't have … He wouldn't. *This doesn't make any sense.* "I didn't think of that."

At school on Monday, Tania chattered on about what to do about Andy, but I couldn't listen. I couldn't. Trent shot me cold, hard glares, and I didn't even care. Whatever.

"Hey, Grace. You okay?" Erica caught up with me outside the cafeteria after lunch. "You seem out of it."

"Just tired, I guess." I managed a smile.

"Okay. See you." She skipped off toward her next class.

Two weeks of rote existence. Mom not talking but muttering. Fuming. Staring out the kitchen window. Ruby holding down the fort, cooking, cleaning up with me. The two of us staring at the Jimmy in the driveway. I didn't ask about the bank account.

Where was he? Had the highway swallowed him up? Had aliens abducted him?

The answer arrived with a ring of the doorbell.

Chapter Fifteen

RUBY HAD PICKED me up from school, and we'd gone shopping at Pepper's Boot Shop in town. She'd gotten her paycheck and desperately wanted a new pair of kicker boots. She found the perfect pair—black with red stitching. They were amazing on her legs. *Bitch.* I tried on a couple of pairs for the heck of it. I put a pair of caramel brown boots with turquoise stitching on my mental wish list.

We finally got home. I was starving. I tossed my school bag on a chair in the kitchen and threw open the fridge door looking for that box of chocolate-covered doughnuts we'd bought at the supermarket yesterday. They weren't my favorite, but a doughnut was a doughnut.

"What's all this?" murmured Ruby, staring at the kitchen table, which was strewn with documents.

My mother sat in a chair, her eyes rooted on something faraway in the distance. I dropped the doughnut box on the counter, my hunger drowning in a choppy ocean of sour. I flipped over a large white envelope and blinked. From a lawyer in Montana.

Ruby snatched the envelope from me. "That fuck."

"Ma?" I said. She remained motionless. "Mom? You

okay?" I crouched by her chair. Her face was pale, her eyes red.

"No. I don't know," she replied, her voice a hoarse whisper.

"That shithead!" Ruby sifted through the papers. "You've got to be fucking kidding me!" she exploded.

"They were delivered an hour ago," fell from Mom's lips.

"What is it? Rube?" I asked.

My mom's gaze met mine. I saw her lips open to say words I knew were coming, and in that split second that she drew breath, a hard, cold collar choked me at the throat. "He's divorcing me."

"What?"

"Your father took off for work and didn't come home. Not one phone call or explanation. And we sat here and worried about him. We called hospitals. That pig!"

"Wow. Wow." Ruby shook her head, bitterness twisting her lips as she scanned the documents.

"He must have been planning this for a long while," my mother continued. "A long while. Must have saved up money and found a place to live. Maybe he even has another family in Montana. You never know."

"Wait, what?" My breathing picked up, and I couldn't catch up. My chest hurt. Ruby stuffed a wad of papers in my face. I grabbed onto a letter, a form, struggled to make sense of the legalese, *"...all property..."* I gulped. "We get the house?"

"Fucking dick," Ruby slammed the papers onto the table, and I flinched.

"Real generous of him, don't you think?" said Mom. "He's washing his hands clean of us, isn't he?"

"Good fucking riddance. We don't need him," said Ruby.

Mom's heavy gaze landed on Ruby and me. "He's still your father."

Ruby shrugged. "He's gone, Mom. Gone! He doesn't want

us, and you know what? I don't want him either. Time to move on. He obviously has."

"Ruby!" I said.

"Look, I know it's a shock," Ruby continued, her eyes gleaming. "But come on …it's better than all the goddamn misery of…"

"Don't," I cut in.

Mom and Dad's relationship had taken a volatile turn after the death of our brother. They both blamed each other for his accident, they both blamed themselves. Neither one was especially emotionally forthcoming—a phrase I'd recently learned in psych class—and it had become easier for each to slump in his corner of the boxing ring of marriage. And we'd all gotten used to it. Like we'd gotten used to the rusty swing set still in the backyard. Jason's swing set. We left it there. We tiptoed around it. We ignored it.

But now Dad had done something about it.

I brought Mom a glass of water, but she only flicked on her lighter and lit a cigarette, inhaling deeply. "Of course, now that you girls are both over eighteen, there won't be any money from him."

Ruby let out a loud, dark laugh, clapping her hands together. "Of course. Wow. He really did plan his escape with precision, didn't he?"

"He did." Mom sat back in her chair, exhaling a stream of thick smoke.

I watched the two of them, I listened. I was at the movies. At the theater. A family drama was playing out before me. *This isn't real. This can't be real.*

My breaths came faster. But I couldn't get much air.

Ruby gestured at me. "He waited until Gracie's birthday, didn't he? It's been what—two weeks, maybe?" Ruby plucked a cigarette from Mom's pack and clicked hard on the lighter, tossing it on the table. "Oooohhhh. I think I'm really impressed now."

My skin flared with heat, a burning heat I couldn't escape from. I was rooted to the spot. The smoke from their cigarettes enveloped the room in a haze, a haze of I didn't know what the hell was going on, I didn't know. I didn't know.

My mother's face came into view. "Baby girl, you okay?"

She blurred. My breaths grew louder, deeper, they weren't a part of me anymore.

"Grace!" Ruby's arms went around me, she hustled me over to the sofa, and my mom came running, a wet glass of water in my hand. "Drink some water, come on. That's it."

The cool liquid slid down my burning throat, dribbled down my lips, my throat. "Dad's gone, Dad's..."

"Yes, honey," murmured Mom, rubbing my cheek with her cold hand. "No note or anything, no phone call. He's not coming back. I'm sorry."

"I'm not sorry," said Ruby.

Mom shot her a look. "Ruby—"

"It'll be fine, Gracie," said my sister, taking my clammy hand in her warm one. "I know this sucks right now, right this minute, it cuts, but it's the truth."

The truth. I'd been deluged with lots of cutting truths lately. This one was the deepest gash of all.

"We'll be okay. We've come this far," Ruby continued. "It's not like we're little kids and don't know what's going on, stressing out Mom. Fuck him."

It was so easy for her, but I couldn't brush off Dad, curse him, and be done with it, tossing him out of my life like an empty potato chip bag. He was DAD.

"We've got each other." Ruby squeezed my shoulders, planting a kiss on my cheek. "Always."

"That's right," said Mom. "Your great-grandma survived a wagon train to get out here. She lost babies, lost her husband in a gold mine, handled men who tried to seduce her out of her property, cheat her. And she survived them all.

That's the stuff we're made of. Right there." She tapped me on my chest over my heart.

"Great-Grandma Rose…" I murmured.

"That's right, honey. Those weren't just old family fairy tales I used to tell you when you were little girls. They're all true. Rose was a tough, strong, smart, sassy woman. And so are both of you. You don't need a man to survive. Just your wits and a lot of heart and soul."

"Mom." I fell into my mother's tight embrace. I never wanted to let go. I wanted to believe in fairy tales again.

"I feel like a fool, though," Mom said on a rough sigh, her hand ruffling through my hair. "All this time, I thought maybe things were getting better. He seemed like he was home more than usual, more talkative, easygoing. I figured he was trying. How stupid was I? He was relaxed because he was counting down the days. He must have been laughing at me the whole time, dying to get out here already."

"He's a heartless, selfish son of a bitch," spat out Ruby.

My mom released me, her hands gently wiping at my face. "I should have up and left a while back, but where we would have gone? Y'all were babies."

"Well"—Ruby stretched out next to me on the sofa, crossing her legs on the coffee table—"we're not babies anymore."

"No, not anymore," Mom said.

There was a buzz in their voices, but I couldn't find my voice. My stomach swam in sour. My blurry gaze found Dad's Jimmy hogging the driveway like it always did. The car in which he taught me how to drive. The car I sometimes got to use to go to school or meet my friends at Drake's for an ice-cream or dinner. I was always so proud of driving that monster thing, which wasn't so much of a monster to me anymore. An old beat-up truck, but it had character. It had been Dad's, and he'd loved it.

"Well, sister, the Jimmy's all yours now," Ruby quipped.

"Yep. It's all there in the documents too," said Mom.

"See? Daddy thought of everything. He took care of everything with one stroke of his pen. What a relief," said Ruby.

Mom wiped her hair back from her face. "The past few years, he'd show up, expect clean laundry, dinner, some small talk, do a few chores around the house, and then go off and do his thing, which meant being gone."

"We're better off." Ruby slid an arm around my shoulders. "You'll see, Gracie."

Mom turned and met Ruby's gaze. Her eyes were clear. She laid a steady hand on Ruby's and gripped tightly. "I agree, honey. We'll be better off." A smile ticked the edges of her lips. Relief. Hope. Confidence.

A shiver licked through me.

They were both caught up in this high. The bandage had been ripped off, and they'd survived the sting. They were pouring shots and knocking them back, relishing the rush. How soon until the throb of pain and anger got loud and fierce again, though? Would Mom be hitting the bottle harder once this surge of self-righteousness had worn off and was replaced with sadness and emptiness?

The two of them chattered on, Mom absently rubbing my leg. It was nice the three of us sitting on the sofa together sharing, it was nice the three of us in the same boat, reaching out and holding onto each other. *We had each other, we'd be good. We were better off. A new chapter for us.*

They talked a good game.

But the boat we were rowing had serious cracks in it. Cracks they kept ignoring. It filled with water, and I always tried to shovel the water out while they rowed on, navigated on without a map or a chart. They rowed on.

Danger, Will Robinson. Danger.

Ruby gripped our mother's hand and mine. "It'll be fun, the three of us."

"You don't live here anymore," I said.

"So? Don't be a party pooper. I'll come spend the night when I can, and you come to Rapid and we can have lunch or dinner, go shopping. Whatever you want."

Whatever I want? I wish I freaking knew what that was. All I knew was that I wanted my daddy back. The daddy I wished I'd had for years now. And now it was too late. Maybe I could have done or said something earlier to make him realize…

Ruby smoothed a hand down my hair. "You feel better? You look better. Got your color back."

"Yeah. Better," I lied.

Maybe I looked better, but my insides were ripped-up live electrical cables, their chopped ends thrashing, sparks hissing wildly.

Chapter Sixteen

GRADUATION CAME AND WENT. No call from Dad. Nothing. Mom and Ruby were there all dressed up. Mom even had a bouquet of white flowers for me, which made me roll my eyes. It was sweet, though. Thoughtful.

"Congratulations, baby. I'm so proud of you." She hugged me, and we held onto each other.

"Thanks, Mom."

In the days that followed, Tania dragged me to all the parties everyone was having, the swimming trips to the reservoir. Alternate waves of emotion washed through me. Free and easy. Tight and numb. Dad was gone, vanished into the ether. And suddenly, high school was over.

Over.

Now what?

While everyone was talking about plans for their "best summer ever," I only saw a long, endless road ahead of me. A road that didn't end anywhere. My deposit for school had been paid, but neither me or Mom sat down and calculated what a school year's worth of expenses would look like. I couldn't bring myself to face it alone. A cold slime slithered through my insides at the thought.

I knew there was no money for me. What little Mom made went into food, utilities, basic expenses. The house. Last month the three of us had to pool our money to get a new hot water heater. We ate spaghetti or eggs for two weeks after that.

"I'm so ready to leave South Dakota. I guess because I never have. Can't wait," Tania said as we got in her car to go swimming with a bunch of friends. Our small coolers, filled with our favorite pop and snacks, were tucked in the backseat.

"Watch out Chicago—Miss South Dakota Farm Girl is comin' fer ya!" I shouted out the window as we left Meager behind.

"Woohoo!" Tania shouted, hitting the gas hard, and we both laughed. "It'll be so amazing to be on my own for the first time," she said. "No Mom telling me what to do. No Penny with her complaining and constant dramas. No hyper little brother to babysit and put up with. Oh my God, I can't wait. And you have to come visit me as soon as you can."

"Hmm," was my only response, my feet up on her dash, my gaze on the blur of prairie grasses whipping by us on the road.

I hadn't told her that I didn't think I'd be going to school. I couldn't spit it out into the world yet. I kept all that bolted inside me. I couldn't think about it. Not yet.

We finally got to the Hippie Hole and sucked on cold bottles of iced tea as we trekked through the rocky path to the water hole hidden in a cluster of towering granite formations. The heat and humidity had made my skin sticky. The Hole was crowded, but we managed to find a patch of ground for our towels and stuff. We jumped in the water right away. The water was brisk, shocking perfection. We found our friends. Some of the girls screeched when the guys splashed water on them. They didn't dunk their bodies all the way in the water, they floated on top, their nipples showing through their tiny bikini tops. I guess that was the plan.

After a quick swim, I pulled up on a slab of stone and

dried off in the sun. I closed my eyes and breathed in the fresh pine scent around me. Rough, male laughter barreled from overhead. Slanting my head to see better, I squinted. A bunch of muscly, long-haired guys were packing up their stuff. I recognized the tall guy with the long braid. It was Jump, the One-Eyed Jack from the keg party. I recognized the other Jacks too. A group of solid masculinity. No nonsense males. I pulled my legs in tighter. Was that Jack who'd brought me Ruby, the one with those caramel-colored eyes, who I'd talked with, up there? He had to be, but I didn't see him.

They were picking up their towels and beer bottles, stuffing their trash in a plastic bag. I guess they were leaving. Several women were with them too.

"Hey! Cut the shit!" My pulse kicked up. *That voice.* My head turned again, and I sat up straighter as if that would help me see better. A bare-chested guy holding a duffel bag turned as someone tossed beer cans at him. He cursed and roared with laughter. It was *him*. His messy dark blond hair shook in his face, his long, bare arms flexing. He had tattoos on his arm, a huge one around his middle. Was that a snake?

"You ever get into trouble?" came roaring back at me, and a flash of heat flared through me.

Nope, not me.

The Jacks didn't have any concerns about what they were supposed to be doing. They hung out and had fun, didn't they? Wasn't that was club life was all about? Life on the edge of 'normal'? Normal kind of sucked from where I sat. One of the girls in a super skimpy bikini jumped on his back, and they both laughed. He hitched her into a better position and carried her out of view. The Jacks were gone.

I didn't want to be stuck in this dry prairie of emotion anymore, but I felt empty. Drained. Immobile. It was mid-August already. People would be leaving for school by next week.

I got home from the Hippie Hole, and Mom's small suitcase greeted me at the front door. "Mom?"

"Hi, honey bee, guess what?" Mom wore her dark mauve lipstick and eye makeup. I hadn't seen her in a full face of color in a long time. She looked good. "Tammy won a weekend away at a casino hotel at the Rosebud Reservation."

"Really?" I dumped my backpack in the kitchen and grabbed the orange juice.

"Really! We're going with Lanie too. The three of us are going to have a wild girls' weekend."

I wiped the juice from my lips. "Wow. Lucky you."

"It'd be nice to get lucky, that's for sure."

"For Pete's sake, Janet."

"Oh, come on, Gracie."

"You're leaving already?"

"Tammy's picking me up now. I'm so excited."

"Good for you. You need this. It'll be fun." My gaze fell on a glass of whiskey on the kitchen table. Guess she'd decided to catch a buzz for the road trip.

"Damn straight, I need it. And I will make sure and have plenty of fun. I told Ruby. She's coming to spend the weekend here. I don't want you to be alone."

"I'm a big girl now, Mom."

"Yes, you are."

A horn honked from outside. "That's Tammy." Mom hustled to the front door and grabbed at the handle of her suitcase. "Bye, baby. I'll give you a call when we get there, okay?" She kissed me, and I opened the front door wide for her.

I waved at Tammy, and she waved back. My mom threw her bag in the car's trunk and slammed it shut. She waved at me once more as she got in the front seat. They took off.

The house all to myself would be a Godsend. I picked up Mom's glass of whiskey and sipped on it, its heat searing my mouth, burning my throat, warming my belly. I prayed Ruby would forget to come over. It was Friday after all, and she usually had big plans on the weekends.

But I was wrong.

So wrong.

Chapter Seventeen

RUBY CAME OVER ALL RIGHT. With her new boyfriend.

"He's not my boyfriend," she'd told me last week. "We're sleeping together." He was a bartender at the bar in Sturgis where she'd gotten a job this summer for Rally season. Ruby and her non-boyfriend showed up at three in the morning along with another guy.

I was still awake. Having gone to the movies earlier with Tania to see "Ghost," I'd fallen into a Patrick Swayze swoon mood, so when I got back home, I fished out our old videos of "Dirty Dancing" and "The Outsiders." "Outsiders" was finishing when the door opened, and Ruby and the two guys strode in. I slid up on the sofa. They were carrying paper bags with bottles.

"This is my sister, Grace," she said over her shoulder as she headed into the kitchen. "Grace, this is Tony, and this is Jonathan."

"Hey," they each said. They were attractive. Tony had longish curly dark hair and dark eyes, Jonathan sported a buzz cut as if he'd been in the military.

"Hi."

Out of the paper bags and onto the kitchen table came

different bottles of booze. Tony made cocktails using the juice we had in the fridge.

"Gracie, you want a tequila sunrise? Tony's very talented with his cock … tails." She burst into a roll of laughter. "Ver-rrrrry talented." Tony grabbed her, and he sucked on the side of her throat like a vampire, his hands digging in her hair.

"No, I'm good. Thanks," I said.

Jonathan came over with a glass of amber liquid. His eyes were glassy. "There's whiskey too. Here, you want some?"

"No, thanks."

He offered me the glass. "It's just whiskey. I promise. And it's the good stuff too. We took a bottle from the bar." He winked at me. "Try it."

I took the glass and sipped the vaporous liquor. It was lighter in color than the stuff Mom and Dad used to drink. The rich liquid enveloped my mouth. Sort of sweet, warm, and oaky. My tongue swiped at my bottom lip as I put the glass down on the table.

"What do you think?" He gestured at the glass as he settled on the far corner of the sofa.

"This is different, better. You were right."

"Top tier Irish whiskey." Jonathan's gaze darted to the television screen. "Swayze, huh?"

"Yep," I said on a grin.

"I liked "Red Dawn." You seen that one?"

Tony's loud laugh exploded from the kitchen, and Ruby pounced on him again, kissing him on the mouth. He pushed her back against the wall, and she groaned, their kiss growing even more ferocious. Jonathan shook his head, laughing as he busied himself at the coffee table, rolling pot into a long doobie. He sprinkled white powder over it from another small packet. He was focused and meticulous about the way he treated his goods. The conscientious pharmacist.

Ruby and Tony finally came over with three drinks and

plopped down in between us on the couch. The three of them drank and smoked the doobie.

"Grace, you want a hit?" asked Ruby.

"No, thanks."

The sharp fragrant smoke filled the living room as the movie finished. I rewound the video, and Tony grabbed the remote control and flipped through the TV channels.

"Let's take them now," Ruby squeezed Tony's leg and went into the kitchen. She sifted through small baggies on the table, returned, and handed Tony and Jonathan each a pill, and they popped it in their mouths, chasing it with booze. Was it Ecstasy? A lot of kids were doing it this summer. Made them feel high and happy and … into sex.

Maybe I should try it.

Ruby slid into Tony's lap, and they kissed, then she slid back in between both guys again. Tony had his hand in Ruby's hair. Ruby's hand stroked Jonathan's thigh. Tony stopped his channel-hopping at MTV, and I kept my eyes trained on Michael Hutchence, strutting his stuff, telling me he needed me tonight.

"Gracie, you sure you don't want?" Ruby offered me the last of the burning joint as Tony nuzzled her neck.

"No, it's okay," I said, grabbing the whiskey once more and taking a small sip.

Jonathan took the joint from her fingers as his other hand rubbed Ruby's thigh. I returned my attention to INXS on the TV screen. Soft laughter rose from the sofa next to me. Jarring movement.

"You're bad," whispered Ruby hoarsely.

Was she going to have sex with both of them? Of course she was. *Holy crap. Holy crap.* My skin burned. I was dying to look. I would die if I did.

The sofa pillows jostled against me as the three of them rose. "G'night, Gracie," Ruby's voice warbled. Was it the booze, the drugs? Was it lust?

"Good night," I said, biting my lip. *Good night? Really? Oh, what should I have said, for shit's sake?*

Their footfalls and murmurings disappeared down the hall. I recognized the extended creak of my parents' bedroom door as it swung open, swung shut.

Motherfudgemycake.

Laughter and moans. A heavy groan. Soft slaps. My ears burned with the strain to hear. "Ruby, Ruby, Ruby…" one of them said. "Fuck, yeah," said another. "Oh! Oh! Oh!" "Goddammit" came more. Over and over again.

Over and over.

Quiet. Murmurs. Fumbling. Quiet.

I let out a jagged breath and clicked on VH-1. A Journey retrospective was playing. "Lovin' Touchin' Squeezin'" ripped from the television.

Exactly!

A steady thumping grew stronger. Got faster. Was it mom's bed against the wall? The headboard? Maybe the dresser? Was Ruby on the dresser or—*damn.*

My breathing picked up. I closed my eyes, and my hard nipples—*when did that happen?*—grazed against the fabric of my tee.

A male voice rose, gruff and harsh. "Fuck, Ruby, fuck, so good. Like that, yeah like that. Look at her, man, look at my dirty girl taking us both. Ah fuck, yeah."

What exactly was Ruby doing? *How* was she doing it? How the heck was she keeping track? My imagination ran wild. Maybe you didn't keep track, you only felt and did and felt and did. I took another sip of the whiskey as I tucked my legs underneath me on the sofa, squirming.

An animal-like howl rose from the bedroom and low moans. Goosebumps flicked over my skin, my fingernails dug into my flesh. Murmurings. Sated groans woven with soft cries.

I envied my sister. I really did. I envied her wildness. Her sense of freedom. Her pushing her own envelope. Her knowing what she wanted and getting it, her daring to try new things. All the things, apparently. The bedroom door creaked open, and the bathroom door opened and shut. I waited. Doors opened and closed once more. Footsteps. Soft voices. The squeaky creak of that bedroom door final.

I shut down the TV, the lights, made sure the front door was locked. I got to my room and threw myself on my bed. My white curtains fluffed in the slight breeze against my open window, a window that Ruby had climbed through so many nights when she was my age, having long missed her curfew after a long night of drinking or smoking pot at someone's house usually with Deke, fooling around with Deke, and then with Tim and whoever else. She'd whisper all the details as I'd help her get undressed, and eventually, we'd both fall asleep.

Now there was no Mom or Dad to hide from. No curfews, no forbidden anything.

I curled into a ball, tugging my quilt higher over my shoulder. The house was quiet. So quiet. Were Ruby, Jonathan, and Tony asleep now? How were they sleeping? All three of them entangled in each other's sweaty, naked bodies? Or were two of them doing it quietly while the third slept or maybe while the other watched and stroked himself or he…

My pulse throbbed, my skin heated.

Sliding my hand under my pajama waistband, I touched myself and found wetness. My hips rocked in a pleading rhythm as my fingers swirled and stroked. My breath caught, sounds escaped my lips. My body tightened, my chest constricted. I wanted to come. I wanted to come so bad. I hadn't been able to make myself come for months now. My brain seemed to invade right when I got close, right at the exact moment when…

Dammit. Like that. Flatline.

I buried my face in my pillow.

———

Ruby and the guys spent the whole weekend at the house, coming over late again on Saturday night after they all got off work. Tony made amazing western omelets and french toast. Jonathan used Dad's tools he'd found in the garage and fixed the leaky faucet in the bathroom.

Mom called once to say she and her friends were having a blast and wouldn't be back until Monday. I went to my summer job at Tibbet's Grocery that Mom's friend, Lanie owned and helped out the tourists, who were still pouring through the Black Hills for Sturgis Rally season, even though the rally had finished a couple of weeks ago. Water bottles, pop, beer, every snack in the book. Cigarettes. Maps. Meager was actually crowded this time of year. A steady stream of people on bikes rolled through town, stopping to eat, shop. Ask directions. All the biker tourists were real friendly and thrilled to be in South Dakota. In August, we were no longer a blip on the map. We were an "ultimate destination" for thousands.

"Here's your change," I said, handing the dollar bills and coins to the older man with a faded bandana around his head and a long, fluffy white beard. He had to be pushing sixty-something.

"Thanks, honey."

"You're welcome. Are you enjoying your ride through the Black Hills?"

"Oh, you bet we are. You're so lucky to live here, young lady. This area is something else. So much to see. Real unique country. We're loving it."

"Where are you from?"

"We came all the way from Pittsburgh to be here," said his wife, taking the six-pack of cola and cigarettes in hand. "Nothing like riding out here in South Dakota. This has been our bucket list trip for so long."

"Wow, really?" I replied. "I'm glad you're having a great time then."

"We are. The best. We're heading to the Badlands now," she said, sliding her sunglasses on.

"Have a great time. Thanks again."

Husband and wife left the store, and I stared after them as they got on their massive Harley trike. I couldn't imagine riding on a bike all the way across the country. She put her arms around his waist, and the bike roared to life, the two of them grinning. They were happy, in tune with each other and their shared passion for riding and traveling. Simple, really. If only my parents had shared a few mutual hobbies. Other than arguing and blaming.

Early Sunday evening, after I got off work, I pulled the Jimmy up in the driveway as Tammy and Mom stood at the front door. I didn't expect them until Monday morning.

"Hi Mom. You're back early, huh?"

"Yes, we are," said Tammy, her smile strained.

"Goddamn motherfucking—" Mom grumbled, jostling the doorknob, keys in her fist. She couldn't get the lock open.

"Let me get that for you, Mom. I'll do it." I took the keys from her hand and inserted the right one, and did the push-pull-shove on the door that was needed to open it. The door popped open.

"Finally!" Mom stumbled into the house.

Tammy's eyebrows raised up. "Your mom had a little too much to drink."

"Oh."

"I mean, she had too much the whole time," Tammy stage-whispered. "She got loud and mean at one point, ranting a lot about your dad. It got to be a problem."

I shifted my weight under Tammy's stare. "I'm sorry."

"She's going through a rough patch, I get it. It's not easy." Tammy squeezed my arm. "I'll leave you to it, sweetie." She got back into her car and took off.

My gaze followed my mother staggering down the hall to her bedroom. *Oh shit.*

"Why is my room such a goddamn mess? What the hell happened? Was there an earthquake? Grace! Did you two have a party? Jesus! I'm going to kill Ruby!"

I stepped into the house and yanked at the front door. It slammed behind me with a boom.

But I didn't flinch.

The screw, that long, thick screw that had been drilling in my insides for months, bore deeper inside me. The cold metal twisted tighter at my center, searing me raw with its ice. Drilling me into the floor right into the ground.

There was no way I could leave home.

And I'd known it all along.

Chapter Eighteen

THERE WAS no coffee maker making coffee in the kitchen, which was totally odd. The first thing Mom did in the morning was head for the machine, load it up, and stare at it until it was ready. The house was freezing in the mornings. It was November, and we'd already had two major snowstorms. You needed hot coffee first thing. I'd never cared much for coffee before, but now I couldn't live without it, especially when I had the morning shift at work.

My gaze fell on two glasses of liquor on the coffee table in the living room.

Her bedroom door creaked open, and I turned at the sound, tipping my head. Footsteps. But it wasn't Mom. It was a man. A man I knew. I froze.

"Morning," he said.

All circuits down.

"I'm just going to—" He pointed to the front door, a hand smoothing down his faded plaid flannel shirt over his round middle.

"Uh-huh."

My former math teacher tracked past me through the living room, darting out the front door.

My pulse—the only part of me that functioned—ticked in my neck. He shut the door, and I blinked. My gaze followed him through the living room window. He slipped on the driveway, righted himself, and darted to his car parked on the side of the road.

"Mom?"

"You're here?" came her sharpened voice from her bedroom.

"Yes, I'm here. What the hell was that?"

"What?"

"Mr. Raines strolling through our house? I saw him, Mother."

Janet emerged from the hall, pulling the belt on her robe tight, her hair up in a ponytail, lips pursed. She swanned past me, making a beeline for the kitchen. "He's very nice."

Mom had been going to Pete's, our local bar, every Tuesday night without fail. Tuesday was Ladies Night, and she and Tammy and Lanie took full advantage. This was the first time she'd brought a man home. I didn't even realize she'd been sleeping with men.

"You know him?" sputtered out of my mouth.

"Well, now I do." She sent me a smirk over her shoulder as she poured spoonfuls of coffee in the machine. "It's not the first time Doug and I have … you know. But it's the first time you've been around in the morning to see, that's all."

My mouth dried. She'd been bringing Mr. Raines home? Maybe other men too? Sure, I wanted her to date and be happy, but … I don't know. My mother had a whole other life going on suddenly. "Oh," was all I could manage.

"Don't give me that tone of voice, Gracie. Should I be a nun now?"

"No, I didn't mean that, Mom."

"Your father certainly isn't being any kind of monk, the pig."

Word had gotten back to Mom that Dad had a girlfriend. Or maybe he was only on some date at this bar in North Dakota. Who knew. Didn't matter. He was seen *canoodling* with another woman, as it was told to Mom. That was enough. Now Janet was in fifth gear, taking her laps around that track, catching up.

"Isn't Mr. Raines married?" I asked.

"Mr. Raines is not getting it at home, which is a shame because he … anyhow." She cleared her throat as she took down a mug from the cupboard and set it down on the counter. "You want a cup?"

My stomach roiled, a sour stew sloshing away in the pit of my being. "No. I'll stop by Drake's on the way to work."

"Suit yourself."

I should suit myself. Seemed like everybody else was.

"By the way, did you pick up the bags of salt we'd talked about yesterday?" I asked. "There's bad ice all over the driveway again. In fact, Doug slipped on it on the way to his car."

"What?" she lit a cigarette, settling into her chair.

"You said you were going to get the salt, Ma. The driveway…"

"I didn't have a chance. You go."

"But, Mom, I have to get to work and—"

"Can't you go to the hardware store in town and grab a few bags? We'll go to the Save-Mart another time. My head's killing me, I can't right now."

I knew if I didn't do it, it would not get done, and the ice on the driveway and our walkway would only build. And if I didn't de-ice the driveway now, she would slip and fall, or our cars would slide, lose control, like hers did only last week, ramming into our neighbor's Nova. Mom had been drinking, but I managed to blame it on the ice on the driveway, and our next-door neighbors, Bill and Karen, didn't say much. They knew, though. Who didn't?

I shoved on my boots. "So, how many margaritas did you have last night?"

She blew out a plume of smoke, grabbing the bottle of ibuprofen she kept out on the table. "No margaritas. Shots—we did Sex on the Beach shots." She sucked down two tablets with her coffee. "They were real yummy."

She was always a wine drinker or wine spritzers or those new flavored wine coolers. Now she was doing shots. Shots with men. *My mother and Mr. Raines were downing fucking shots at a bar and getting it on.*

The phone rang. "Answer that, would you?" She gulped down coffee as she flipped through the supermarket sales flyer I'd left on the table yesterday.

I picked up the cordless phone I'd left in the entryway. "Hello?" I went to the coat tree and grabbed my jacket.

"Gracie? It's Dad."

My heart leaped like a baby deer onto a busy highway. Holding my breath, I shuffled around the corner so Mom couldn't have an eye view of me from the kitchen. "What is it?" I asked.

"I wanted to say happy Thanksgiving."

"It's not Thanksgiving yet."

"Well, I thought it might be better to call today, the day before, if you all were going to—"

"Maybe it's better for you? You'll be busy, huh?" I whispered. "Is your new girlfriend cooking for you? Or are you taking her on a holiday vacation? Skiing in Aspen? Cruise to the Bahamas?"

"Who is it, Grace?" Mom shouted from the kitchen, and my spine tightened at the reminder of her presence. A reminder to keep my cool.

"I got it, Mom. It's for me." I ground the receiver into my ear.

"She's there?" Dad said.

"It's her house, isn't it?"

"How's college, Gracie?"

He might as well have slapped me in the face, poured ice-cold water over me. But I didn't feel the sting. I didn't feel the wet.

There was no college.

I couldn't leave Meager with Mom sinking more and more into alcohol and odd behavior with each passing week. She was up, she was down. Ruby went from one job to the next, one apartment to the other, or she'd crash at some friend's house for a few days. Last week, she followed some rock group out to Minneapolis. I was still waiting to hear from her. Neither she nor Mom even noticed that I hadn't packed up and left for school. August had rolled into September into October, and here we were in November.

Here I was.

"Oh, college is great, Dad. Thanks for asking. Are we done now?"

"Gracie, come on—"

"What do you want from me, Ray? This is the first time we've heard from you since you ditched us months ago. What do you want me to say?" My voice had transformed into something strong and clear.

"Fine. I—"

Fine? A snake uncoiled, hissing, sizzling, revealing its fangs.

"Here's what I want to say, Dad. What you did hurt. It still hurts. You didn't have to do it like that. You didn't." My voice quaked. I didn't want it to. I wanted to be strong. Tough. "It was wrong," I breathed fire.

My blurry gaze fell on the old cowboy riding a horse statue on the hallway table that had been there since before I was born. Dad's fake Remington. It was time to get rid of that thing and get something I liked for the hallway. That's right. I would do that today, goddamn it.

Dad dragged out a long breath. "Look, I just wanted to wish you and your sister—"

"Yeah, great. Got it." I clicked the phone off. My breaths came fast and short as if I'd sprinted a race. The blood charged through my veins. I was going to explode. I needed to get a grip.

I told him. I'd actually told him how I felt. Would it make a difference to him? I'd never know. But that ache in my chest was still there, still twisting. I shoved it in deeper. I squelched it. My forehead sank against the wall.

"Who was that, Gracie?" Mom's voice rang out.

My body straightened. I released my death grip on the phone and dropped it on the table next to the stupid cowboy statue. "Nobody."

Chapter Nineteen

"COME ON, COME ON, COME ON..." I pleaded with the Jimmy. I'd parked a block down from the hardware store in front of Dillon's, bags of salt in the back.

I turned the ignition. Nothing. This was already a shitty crappy morning to end all mornings. I needed to get home and salt the driveway and then get to work. Not this too. Please, please, not the truck.

I tried again. Again, nothing. "Dammit!"

Taking in a deep breath, I stared out the windshield. Clay Street was crowded with people last-minute shopping for tomorrow. The big display window of Dillon's had its annual Thanksgiving wonderland scene set up. Figurines of Pilgrims, Natives, pumpkins, and turkeys all set up artfully in a field of corn along with colorful paper fall leaves tacked onto the glass. That holiday window had not changed since I was a little girl. There was something comforting in that. Something annoying.

My fingers tightened over the key in the ignition once more as I closed my eyes and bit my bottom lip. "Please, please, God. Let me get home with the stupid salt before Janet decides to go out into the driveway with nothing but her robe on and slips or decides to go out with the car and…"

A sharp knock on my frosted, drippy window interrupted my plea, and I jerked in my seat, my fingers gripping the steering wheel. A tall guy with a short beard and a distinct jawline stood over me.

I rolled down the window a crack. "Yes?"

He leaned into me. "Hey, you having car trouble?" came a rough, almost hoarse voice. Hoarse in that casual rugged Kris Kristofferson kind of way.

I knew who this guy was. I'd never seen him close up before, but I'd seen him cruising around town many times on an impressive and very noisy old Harley. He was a One-Eyed Jack.

My fingers slid down the steering wheel to the bottom. "It's … nothing. Thanks. It's okay."

He slanted his head, slight crinkly lines around his eyes and forehead deepening as he squinted at me from behind dark aviator sunglasses. He was one of the older Jacks in the club. "You sure about that?" he asked, his raspy voice mellow.

"Yeah … it … um…"

A grin tipped the edges of his lips. "Uh-huh, go on."

I pressed back into my seat. "It won't start. It does that a lot. No biggie. Thanks for asking, though." I started rolling up my window.

He stopped it with his fingers. "I fix cars and bikes for a living. Maybe I can help." He removed his sunglasses, settling them on his head. Startling blue eyes gleamed at me. He wasn't taking no for an answer. His big hand thumped on the side of the Jimmy. "I remember this truck. Hard to forget this color."

"You do? From where?"

"From my club." He eyed me, head slanted. "Was that your dad that came up to the club a while back after that party?"

"Oh. Yes." My face heated. "That was my dad."

"Were you the—"

"She was the little sister," came a deep voice that jolted right through me. Another guy appeared next to the Jack. Messy locks of dark blond hair, honey brown eyes. It was *him*, the Jack who'd saved Ruby. A killer grin flashed over his face. Killer as in …

Holy cow.

He lifted his chin. "Hey there. How are you?" His voice was as rich and gruff as I remembered, and my insides heated and curled like paper on fire at the sound.

"Hi. I'm good." I slid up my seat. *Shit, thank God I put some makeup on this morning.*

He turned to the other Jack. "I'm going to go pick up our order at Marla's. Be right back." He sauntered down the sidewalk toward Marla's Eatery, the cold glow of the winter sun highlighting that mop of hair and the big Jacks skull patch on the back of his leather jacket. Suddenly, his head turned back, and he held my gaze. My heart stopped. That grin slowly warmed his features once more, but this time, it was, I don't know, *gentle*. My skin heated. Everything heated. He turned around again and took my breath with him down the sidewalk.

"So, little sister—"

My head jerked. "Sorry, what?"

"My name's Wreck, by the way."

"I'm Grace."

"Pretty name."

"Thanks."

"You going to let me look under the hood here, Grace?"

Oh, what the hell. "Sure." I yanked at the lever to pop the hood and got out of the Jimmy. Wreck studied the engine, the hoses. He inspected, his fingers brushing over valves and connections.

"You know, at that party? The guys were great," I said.

His blue eyes lifted to mine. "They're good men." Those eyes seemed to brighten, and it was an arresting sight. There was clarity there. A kind of contentment. It was soothing.

He went back under the hood. "This puppy needs some work. Not to mention new tires now that winter's here. The roads are clear today, but—"

"I should've taken care of that sooner, I know." I tugged on my hair. I hated people thinking I was reckless or irresponsible, because I wasn't. Not me. But getting a new set of tires for the truck would be a lot of money. A heck of a lot.

"So your dad gave you the truck?"

"Actually, he left it behind when he took off. It's mine now," my voice snapped.

"Oh. Sorry to hear that. He seemed…" He took in a breath, thought better of what he was about to say. "Well, anyhow."

"Yeah."

"You and your sister doing okay? Your mom?"

"We're fine." I jammed my hands deep into my jacket pockets. "I graduated from high school, live at home, and work the cash register at Tibbet's, while most of my friends are away at college, having a blast and getting on with their lives. Life's great." My voice was acrid. I was acrid. I guess it was easy to express my emotions to a complete stranger. How screwed up was that?

He only squinted his dark blue eyes at me. "You wanted to go to school but—"

"I got into one, but with my dad leaving, I wasn't able to go all the way to Denver. Anyhow, I figured I should stick around. Help out my mom and stuff."

"That's a good choice then. Won't be forever, right?"

"I guess not, no."

"But it kinda sucks right now, huh?" He rubbed at his jaw.

"Yeah, it does."

"You feeling left behind?"

I held his intense blue gaze. "I do," I breathed. I'd never admitted that to anybody, even myself.

"I get that." He turned away, sniffing in air, his lips slowly tucking into a slight grin. "Hey, if not Denver, somewhere else maybe. Somewhere that fits into your new situation. You looking into it?"

I shifted my weight. "Uh, no, not yet."

"You should get on that if that's what you want."

"True." My teeth scraped my lip.

"So, Grace, why don't you come by my repair shop, and I'll work on the truck. I could replace a few—"

My face flushed, my jaw dropped, and I picked it back up speedily as if it were my panty that had fallen out of my pocket onto the sidewalk. "Um … at the clubhouse?"

"Yeah."

"Oh no. Really. That's all right."

"I might have some spare tires that would work too. I got plenty of odds and ends at my shop. Bring it over and I'll—"

"No, really. That's okay."

I was so tired of people being nice since Dad had left. Giving us the "oh you poor dears" look, and sympathetic voice. I knew that's what this was. It was nice of him to offer, but no, please no. Mom always ate it up because then she could launch into her lengthy laundry list of all the ways that pig, Ray Hastings had done her and her girls wrong.

I hated it. When would this be over?

"Thanks, Wreck, but really, you don't have to."

He hitched a hand on his waist. "Young lady, I don't *have to do anything.*"

"Well, that sure must be nice."

His head rocked back, and he laughed out loud.

My hand went to my mouth. "I'm so sorry. That was rude. I didn't mean—I'm in a mood, I guess. That's no excuse, but—"

"You weren't being rude, honey. You were being real, and that's the only way to be, in my book."

"I wish more people felt that way."

"Grace, it damn well is nice to not have to do what you don't really want. More than nice. I think you should try it sometime."

As if. If only.

He leaned a hand on the Jimmy. "I'd like to help you out. I want to. Tomorrow is Thanksgiving."

I pressed my lips together, biting down on them. *Thanksgiving. Holidays. Who cares? Not me.* My lungs burned. My nostalgia and emotions boiled hard under the metal lid I'd clamped down over them months ago.

"And anyhow, I'd offered to look at this truck when your dad had come over, but he never brought it 'round."

"Seems he had other things on his mind. Would've been nice, though. It would have been in good shape for when he left it behind for me. Guess that was asking too much."

He let out a chuckle. "You got a good sense of humor there. Hang onto it."

I grinned. "Oh, I will."

"We really appreciated the deal he made with everyone on our behalf. 'Cause, let's face it, that would've been a real shitstorm here in town with those dads."

"That is true."

"So, let me do this for you."

"You guys already did a lot, and …" My voice trembled. Emotion shuddered through me, and I was helpless against the tide. I was grateful for his concern. It was the nicest, kindest thing that had happened to me in such a very long time. A spring of water in a dry prairie. "It's very generous of you."

Wreck put a hand on my shoulder and squeezed lightly. "Hey, it's okay. I get it. You've been through a hell of a lot lately. Want to help you out if I can. And *this* I can do." He went to the front of the truck and slammed the hood down firmly. His gaze shot to the Dillon's Thanksgiving Day window and his features tensed. "I'm trying to get into the holiday spirit myself."

A tight silence stretched between us, and his gaze finally returned to me. "Not easy this year, but we need to be grateful for what we got, right? Count our blessings and all that? No matter the cards you've been dealt." He pressed his taut lips together, his gaze searching mine. There was emotion there, but he was experienced at holding it back.

I swallowed hard. "I guess."

"You're cautious. That's good. Smart. Let me help you out, Grace. No strings here."

I wiped at the corner of my eye before anything spilled over and I made more of a fool of myself. "Okay."

"Good. Bring her in as soon as you can. Today, if you want. I'm not going anywhere for the holiday. You come on up anytime, no appointment needed."

My chest tightened at the thought of going up to the Jacks' clubhouse on my own. I'd bet Ruby would want to come with. She'd probably grab my keys and take the Jimmy up on her own.

"Okay."

"Promise?"

"I promise," I said. "I really appreciate this."

"Stop thanking me and get in and try starting her up."

I climbed back in the truck, my palms sweaty on the steering wheel, the stupid key. I turned the ignition. The engine started.

"There she is." He winked at me, wiping his hands together.

"Phew!" I grinned. My muscles finally unwound. "Thank you, Wreck."

"You're welcome. Get yourself home now, and don't take any chances on the road. And until you bring her over, don't take her out of Meager. Getting stuck here in town isn't much of a big deal, but if…"

Ha. I was already stuck in Meager. Me and the Jimmy were stuck here together for life.

"What is it?" he asked. He'd noticed my sour smirk.

"It's nothing."

"All right. Well, I better see this truck in my drive later today, or the day after Thanksgiving, you got that?"

"I got it."

"Good." He thumped his hand on the hood. "Happy Thanksgiving."

"Happy Thanksgiving, Wreck."

He stalked down the sidewalk to a hulking black and chrome bike, which I couldn't see very well because my vision was blurry with a new wave of tears. I wiped furiously at my eyes. I hadn't cried much so far, and I refused to open the floodgates now. One simple act of kindness from a stranger— yet another Jack, in fact—and I was overwhelmed with emotion. *Deep breath in. Deep breath out.* It didn't burn and boil my insides this time. I didn't have to talk it down with a whip like a wild animal. No. It was a great big balloon I'd let go of, and it floated gently in the sky above me.

The loud, loud growl of that Harley ripped through the air and jolted my pulse. The other Jack had returned from Marla's and stuffed a big brown bag from the restaurant into his bike's storage compartment. Easing into his saddle, he revved his own engine with a grin on his face. So much noise. The two Jacks tore down Clay Street together, hair flying in the wind under their small helmets. A smile slowly tipped the edges of my lips. Even in late November they rode their bikes if the roads were clear, damn the cold. They didn't miss an opportunity to experience what they loved so much. They disappeared from view, and my gaze fell back on Dillon's holiday window in front of me.

Thanksfreakinggiving.

The Pilgrims were thankful for their survival and a good harvest. Well, I had the survival part down so far, didn't I? The good harvest, though? Not so sure. But like the Pilgrims, I'd take what pumpkins I could get and make pie out of them.

I let out a laugh. What if I focused on what I did have and not on what I didn't for a change? I was grateful for Wreck reaching out and fixing the truck. I had Mom and Ruby who loved me, cared about me like I loved and cared for them despite their crazy asses. Yeah, they were both going through a rough time of it, each of us was handling it in her own way, but the sting of what Dad had done would fade soon enough, wouldn't it? And then what? I didn't want to be stuck in bitter forever. I didn't. I wanted to get on with my life. I was eighteen years old, for Pete's sake, and I had my whole life ahead of me.

Maybe I could look into schools around Rapid like Wreck suggested. No, it wouldn't be the same as being in Denver, wouldn't be what I'd dreamed of, but it would be *something*, something good I was doing for me. In the time being, I could get a better job too, better than being the freaking minimum wage cashier at the local grocery wearing that God awful bright green apron.

My head fell back against the headrest as I took in the figurines of the Pilgrim families seated along with the Natives at the long tables laden with roast turkey and pie and corn on the cob sculptures. I guess I could be grateful that Dad had bothered to call. I hated him right now, it hurt, but I liked hearing his voice. I was glad he'd reached out. That he'd tried. That was *something*.

And you could build on "something."

I certainly didn't expect anything to change or get better anytime soon. Once crossed or lied to, Ruby and Mom both kept that bitter anger stoked like an eternal flame torch meant to burn forever and ever. Dad's betrayal and abandonment was no small torch, though, but a nuclear bomb, for sure.

Maybe one day he and I could talk regularly on the phone or see each other or …

Who knows, maybe, but I wasn't going to count on it right now, and I sure wasn't going to sit around and wait for it. No, I had to slide my boots back on and march through that cornfield or pumpkin patch or whatever the hell and do whatever it took to make my own harvest happen. Even hunt my own turkeys.

"Geez." I let out a laugh, shaking my head at my hokey Thanksgiving analogies. But it helped. My heart felt lighter. It did. I tore my gaze away from Dillon's and checked in my mirrors as I put the Jimmy carefully in reverse. I swung out of my parking spot and onto Clay Street.

I headed home.

Chapter Twenty

RUBY'S CAR was in the driveway. I parked the Jimmy and tore into the house. She and Mom drank coffee at the kitchen table.

"You're back!"

My sister's bright hazel eyes met mine. "Yep, I'm back. I didn't want to miss Thanksgiving with you and Mom." I tackled Ruby, hugging her hard. "You okay?" she whispered in my ear, rubbing my back.

"Better now." I kissed her cheek, releasing her.

"I brought doughnuts from Wall Drug." She gestured at a box from the famous Black Hills store Mom had opened. "Want some?"

"Are you kidding? Hell yes. The last time we had those, we were what—ten?" I ripped off my jacket and washed my hands at the sink.

"Something like that." Mom handed me a dish with two plump, sugary doughnuts. "Jason loved them. Remember?"

Ruby and I glanced at each other. Mom hadn't mentioned our brother's name in forever.

"Yeah, Ma, I remember," said Ruby softly.

"Oh, hang on." I put my dish on the table and grabbed

the phone from the wall and dialed the grocery. "Lanie? Hi, it's Grace. I can't make it to work today." I didn't allow Lanie to interrupt me. "In fact, I need to quit. Sorry for the short notice, but it can't be helped. Thank you for everything." I hung up the phone, then sat at the table and filled my mouth with yeasty, sweet, soft doughnut.

"What the heck was that about?" asked Mom.

I swiped at my mouth. "I quit."

"Good one," said Ruby. "'Bout time."

"I'm going to find something else, something better, and look into schools around Rapid."

"Good for you, honey," said Mom. "Good for you. You should do that. Absolutely."

"Oh and Rube—Wreck, the One-Eyed Jack who runs the club repair shop?"

Ruby's gaze shot to me, an eyebrow arched. "What about him?"

"He offered to fix the Jimmy. For free. Which is so amazing."

"Very amazing. I can take it up there for you," said Ruby, wiping sugar from her lips. "If you want."

"Would you?" I grinned. "That'd be great. He said anytime—"

"Today good?"

"Today's perfect."

"All righty. Will do." Ruby bit into another doughnut.

"So, Ruby, you sticking around after Thanksgiving?" Mom asked.

"Yep. I got myself a job at Pete's," she replied.

"No way, really?" I wiped my fingers on a napkin. "Cool."

"Very cool."

I sat up straighter, a wave of warmth seeping through me as I lifted up my coffee cup. "Here's to a new beginning, whatever it is," I said.

"Yes." Mom said, her eyes glimmering, raising her mug.

I smiled at her. "It's not champagne, but hey."

"We don't need champagne," Ruby said, her tone subdued.

"No, we sure don't." I held her gaze as she lifted her mug to mine. "We need each other."

"Amen," Mom said and we all clinked our coffee cups together.

My tongue swiped at the sugar mingling on my lips with the salt. "I'm thankful for us, and I love you both, no matter what."

Warm tears slid down my face, and I let them.

Books by Cat Porter

Acknowledgments

So many people, so much love!

To my editor Jenn for making my stories shine through thick and thin, for always being there for me all these years, all the time. To Christina for keeping me true to myself and pushing me toward all the right cliffs for my necessary leaps.

To Lori for another wonderful collaboration on a cover, for translating my idea and vision thang into a crisp, fresh reality. All the love!

To my beta readers of a moment's notice on this surprise book: Alison, Dawn, Jan, Korrie, Larri, Rachel for your messages and excitement, your love and friendship. Special thanks to Jenni for your proofreading. (All the justs, my dear!) I appreciate everyone's time and energy on my stories so very much. Your faith in me has my heart full full full.

To Linda and Alissa of Foreword PR for all your support and navigational skills through the high seas at all times.

To all the book bloggers, readers and reviewers, Twitterers, and bookstagrammers, I thank you for reading and taking the time to write and leave reviews and for generously sharing your book love online with your amazing artistic imagery and kind words.

To my Cat Callers for their passion and enthusiasm. This book was inspired by a short story I'd written for you years ago which happened to fit with Dust so beautifully that I had to go there, and I got us here with so much more. I am very grateful and thankful for you all.

To my family who accepted my crazy a long time ago. To Ellen, Jo, MJ, Kim, Soulla, Nancy, Leylah, Autumn, Carian. Your friendship, laughter, and support mean the world to me.

And Grace, yes you. You lit up my past few months with your bright, strong light and I thank you. I needed you. Always. xx

About the Author

Cat Porter was born and raised in New York City, but also spent a few years in Texas and Europe along the way, which made her as wanderlusty as her parents. As an introverted, only child, she had very big, but very secret dreams for herself. She graduated from Vassar College, was a struggling actress, an art gallery girl, special events planner, freelance writer, restaurant hostess, and had all sorts of other crazy jobs all hours of the day and night to help make those dreams come true. She has two children's books traditionally published under her maiden name.

She now lives on a beach outside of Athens, Greece with her husband, three children, and three huge Cane Corsos, freaks out regularly, still daydreams way too much, and now truly doesn't give AF. She is addicted to reading, classic films, cafes on the beach, the Greek islands, Instagram, Pearl Jam and U2, bourbon she brought home from Nashville and whiskey she brought home from Ireland, and realllllly good coffee. Writing has always kept her somewhat sane, extremely happy, and a productive member of society.

for more more more
www.catporter.eu

Sign up for my CatList
for exclusive content, book news, sales,
special giveaways and offers

Follow me on BookBub & Amazon

Join Cat's Facebook group:

Cat Porter's Cat Callers

See my inspiration photos for my novels on Pinterest

Email me at catporter103@gmail.com

amazon.com/author/catporter

bookbub.com/authors/cat-porter

instagram.com/catporter.writer

facebook.com/catporterauthor

twitter.com/catporter103

pinterest.com/catporter103